Books by **GEORGE HARMON COXE**

Murder with Pictures (1935)
The Barotique Mystery (1936)
The Camera Clue (1937)
Four Frightened Women (1939)
Murder for the Asking (1939)
The Glass Triangle (1939)
The Lady Is Afraid (1940)
No Time to Kill (1941)
Mrs. Murdock Takes a Case
   (1941)
Silent Are the Dead (1942)
Assignment in Guiana (1942)
The Charred Witness (1942)
Alias the Dead (1943)
Murder for Two (1943)
Murder in Havana (1943)
The Groom Lay Dead (1944)
The Jade Venus (1945)
Woman at Bay (1945)
Dangerous Legacy (1946)
The Fifth Key (1947)
Fashioned for Murder (1947)
Venturous Lady (1948)
The Hollow Needle (1948)
Lady Killer (1949)
Inland Passage (1949)
Eye Witness (1950)
The Frightened Fiancée (1950)
The Widow Had a Gun (1951)
The Man Who Died Twice
   (1951)
Never Bet Your Life (1952)
The Crimson Clue (1953)

Uninvited Guest (1953)
Focus on Murder (1954)
Death at the Isthmus (1954)
Top Assignment (1955)
Suddenly a Widow (1956)
Man on a Rope (1956)
Murder on Their Minds (1957)
One Minute Past Eight (1957)
The Impetuous Mistress (1958)
The Big Gamble (1958)
Slack Tide (1959)
Triple Exposure (1959), containing
   The Glass Triangle, The Jade
   Venus, and The Fifth Key
One Way Out (1960)
The Last Commandment (1960)
Error of Judgment (1961)
Moment of Violence (1961)
The Man Who Died Too Soon
   (1962)
Mission of Fear (1962)
The Hidden Key (1963)
One Hour to Kill (1963)
Deadly Image (1964)
With Intent to Kill (1965)
The Reluctant Heiress (1965)
The Ring of Truth (1966)
The Candid Impostor (1968)
An Easy Way to Go (1969)
Double Identity (1970)
Fenner (1971)
Woman with a Gun (1972)
The Silent Witness (1973)

These are Borzoi Books, published in New York by
ALFRED A. KNOPF

THE
SILENT
WITNESS

THE
SILENT
WITNESS

George Harmon Coxe

ALFRED A. KNOPF, New York

1973

THIS IS A BORZOI BOOK
PUBLISHED BY ALFRED A. KNOPF, INC.

Copyright © 1972 by George Harmon Coxe

All rights reserved under International and Pan-American Copyright
Conventions. Published in the United States by Alfred A. Knopf, Inc., New
York, and simultaneously in Canada by Random House of Canada Limited,
Toronto. Distributed by Random House, Inc., New York.

Library of Congress Cataloging in Publication Data
Coxe, George Harmon.   The silent witness.

    I. Title.
PZ3.C83942Sj [PS3505.O9636]   813'.5'2   72–8665
ISBN 0–394–48337–5

Manufactured in the United States of America
First Edition

For
J. RANDOLPHE COX,
REFERENCE LIBRARIAN AT ST. OLAF COLLEGE—
THE COMPLETE LIBRARIAN

THE
SILENT
WITNESS

1

The offices of Esterbrook & Warren occupied the sixth floor of one of the older and less imposing buildings on State Street. The owners had not yet converted to automatic elevators, and the operator who took Jack Fenner to the sixth floor at ten o'clock that late spring Tuesday morning was probably older than the building.

The waiting room, opening directly from the elevator, would have been totally unacceptable to a television director or set designer whose job it was to show the viewer the proper background for one of the more prominent and respected law firms in the city. No more than fifteen by thirty, it had paneled walls of real wood and four end tables that were genuine antiques. But the wall-to-wall carpeting had little nap, the two facing settees were more utilitarian than comfortable.

On the immediate right was a wood-and-glass cage with a panel that slid open to permit two-way communication. This was presided over by a plump brunette of uncertain age who, if not particularly attractive, looked efficient. She nodded when Fenner stated his business, plugged in, spoke briefly. As she did so he glanced at the gilt-lettered walnut plaque at one side listing the partners. Esterbrook, now dead, headed the list. Warren, in his seventies, was next. Of the following twelve names George Tyler was number eleven.

The operator pulled the plug and said: "Mr. Tyler will be out in a minute."

Fenner thanked her but as he turned away he considered the phrasing. Heretofore when he had been summoned he had been directed to Tyler's office; apparently this conference was to take place out here and he wondered why. Fortunately there were no other waiting clients, and he turned to inspect the reading material on the low mahogany table and saw that there was less variety here than at his dentist's: two *New Yorkers*, the newer one a month old, *Forbes, U.S. News and World Report, Barron's*, and a current *Wall Street Journal* whose rumpled pages suggested prior use.

He did not have to wait long. Tyler greeted him with a cheer-ful "Hi, Jack," and shook hands, a neat precise man in his mid-thirties, with short brown hair, dark-rimmed glasses, and a healthy outdoor look. At times a gray-flannel-suit man, he was more informal this morning in dark-brown slacks and loafers and an old brown tweed jacket with chamois elbow patches, which had probably come originally from Brooks or Chipp.

"Let's sit over here." He motioned to one of the settees, settled himself, and then seemed unsure of his opening. He finally said so. "I'm not sure where to start and I may digress but stay with me. There are two clients I'd like you to see. Both potential employers if you're interested. One's in my office"—he paused to glance at his watch—"and the other will be here a bit later. Actually the two jobs have a connection."

Fenner nodded, his dark-green eyes attentive and interested, his lean, angular face and flat-muscled body at ease as he waited.

"You've heard of Haskell & Company?"

"They have a plant south of here?"

"Weymouth."

"Make meters for measuring this and that."

"Among other things. You may also have read in the *Journal* that they are about to be taken over by Allied General Industries. That is if the stockholders vote that way at a special board meeting next Monday."

"That's the conglomerate?"

"Right. Very little cash involved. Basically an exchange of stock. As their attorneys, the chief advantage as we see it is that Haskell has no ready market; it isn't even listed. There is also a stipulation that if a stockholder wishes to sell, or if he dies and his estate has to be settled, the other owners have first crack. With Allied General on the big board there is a ready market should one want to sell some or all his holdings."

He had been watching Fenner closely and now he smiled. "Digression number one. Do you know Mark Haskell?"

"I may have met him once casually, but I've seen him in action. A one-punch nightclub and bar performer, slugging first and hoping friends or the owner will break it up before the other guy has a chance to slug back. Usually that's the end of it because the victim doesn't want publicity, but I understand a couple of times charges were made and the complainant bought off."

"Correct. Now do you know Ben Clayton?"

"By sight. I seem to remember he was married to Haskell's present wife."

"Also correct." Again the smile. "Digression number two. Do you know anything about old man Haskell's long-lost daughter? . . . I didn't think so. It goes like this. Mark is the only child of the old man's first marriage. Later in life he married again and this time there was a daughter—"

"Which makes her Mark's half sister."

"Right. Well, the old man had the reputation of being something of a Tartar. You know the word?"

Fenner grinned. "Sometimes spelled Tatar."

"Others referred to him as an old curmudgeon. In any case the second marriage lasted six or seven years and then one day when old Haskell was away overnight his second wife took off with the daughter. Apparently she'd had all she could take and there was a couple thousand in her checking account and two or three pieces of jewelry.

"Now the old boy, being a proud and arrogant man, never made the slightest effort to find her, or even divorce her. Not until he was hospitalized with an incurable condition and realized he wouldn't be around long. What he did was add a codicil to his will—I don't know whether it was because of conscience, remorse, or senility—which stated that if his daughter could be found within ninety days of his death she was to be recognized as his daughter and heir to twenty-four percent of the company stock, the same as Mark.

"We didn't call you in on that one," he added by way of apology, "because we needed action and plenty of man power. We got an international agency and they did the job. Found her working as a manicurist in a Beverly Hills barber shop."

"No question about her identity?"

"None. She's in my office now. Her mother married again and she took her stepfather's name. Nancy Moore. She can give you the past history if you need it, and I'd rather it came from her. But there is no doubt in our mind that she's the daughter." He paused, brows lifting slightly. "By the way, am I right in assuming you still charge only twenty an hour?"

This time Fenner's grin was quick and genuine. He liked clients who used the word "only." Too many reacted with shock and disbelief when they began to estimate the cost of his services.

"Yeah," he said. "Same as last time. I figured I'd go along with the wage-price freeze thing."

Tyler's grunt was good-natured to show he was aware of the wry humor implicit in the remark.

"Very decent of you. And you can bill us for this conference. If you accept the other assignments you can make your own deal. They can afford you."

"What is it they want? You said there was some connection. You mean between this Nancy Moore and Haskell?"

"No. Ben Clayton. He's due here at eleven but he can wait until you've talked to Miss Moore."

"Why do they need me?"

"They've both been threatened."

"Oh? By whom?"

"Mark Haskell."

Fenner waited, eyes narrowing in thought but nothing changing in his face. He found cigarettes, offered them, and when Tyler refused lit his own. Tyler reached an ashtray from an end table and put it on the settee between them. When Fenner saw he was going to be out-waited he said:

"Is he going psycho or something?"

"Maybe a little—if what I've been told is the truth."

"Okay. But before we get into specifics, *why* is he threatening them?"

"One good reason in each case; two—if my information is correct—with Ben Clayton. I told you about the proposed take-over by Allied General. Haskell wants to block it."

"Why?"

"Because, thanks to a father who had not much longer to live and his influence with the board, he wangled himself a salary of a hundred and twenty-five thousand a year as president of Haskell & Company. Hell, Jack," he added in one more brief digression, "that's more than presidents of some companies forty or fifty times the size of Haskell get. Ben Clayton, who is executive vice-president and does all the work, draws forty-five. If Haskell got fifty he'd be overpaid."

"And?"

"Simple. If the takeover is confirmed he's out on his butt. Oh, he'd still have his share of stock but no job. He's got it in for Ben because Ben organized the takeover although he himself only owns five percent. If Haskell can get his half sister's stock or proxy, he can block the deal. If he gets his wife's ten percent he could put pressure on some of the smaller holders."

He paused, took a small breath and shrugged. "I hadn't intended to go into all this, I mean the breakdown of the stock-holders, but maybe I'd better so you'll see how things stand when you talk to Clayton . . . We'd been trying to get the old man to go public, at least with a substantial part of his holdings. It was the sensible thing to do if only for tax reasons.

"But no. Being the sort of man he was he wouldn't listen. For reasons of his own he left Mark twenty-four percent. The same amount to his daughter if she could be found; if not, that share was to go in a trust—I'll spell that out in a minute. Therefore the forty-eight percent the heirs might own would not give them control of the company. I don't think he wanted Mark ever to be in that position.

"In addition," he said, "the old man was very fond of Marion Haskell and was sure she would straighten out the son. He left her ten percent . . . Ben Clayton and three other retired executives have five percent apiece."

Fenner, who had been adding silently, said: "That's seventy-eight percent."

"Right. Another twelve percent is split several ways, one percent here, two percent there. The old man was a hard task-master and never overpaid anyone but he put a great stock in loyalty. So you have this secretary with one or two percent, another with one; an office manager, I don't know who all; some here, some in Florida . . ."

"Ninety percent."

"We, the firm, have ten percent in trust and can vote it. We hold it for the benefit of grandchildren, if any; otherwise it goes to Municipal Hospital. Haskell has been a small but profitable company but its growth has slowed and we're not impressed with the present management. We'd prefer to get rid of the Allied General stock we'll receive and diversify for the trust."

Fenner put out his cigarette. "Okay. Nancy Moore is holding out her stock and Haskell has been threatening. In what way?"

"First the tires on her car were slashed one night. You could say it was senseless vandalism; it happens all the time. Then she was mugged—"

"She's got a lot of company."

"Except that her handbag was not taken. She went down—two guys from behind she never saw—and was roughed up. One of them said something about this just being a sample and the next time being really rough. Then yesterday morning her car was run off the road on one twenty-eight and luck rather than fancy driving saved her from a serious and perhaps fatal accident. And this time she had a witness. Her boyfriend was with her, driving actually. Deliberate. No way it could have been accidental."

Traces of doubt had begun to filter behind Fenner's still narrowed dark-green gaze. Now he nodded absently and took a small breath.

"It sounds as if you were thinking about a bodyguard."

"Companion would be a better word. I thought if Miss Moore could convince you, you might know of some personable young woman who could be with her from morning until she locked herself in her apartment at night."

"I can think of a couple. But what about this boyfriend? Why can't he stick with her?"

"Because Miss Moore won't allow it. Apparently he's got a nasty temper and she's afraid he'll get himself in a jam. When they got back to town after the accident he started looking for Haskell. Somehow he found him in the University Club bar having a pre-dinner drink. He told him off; said any more threats, even over the phone, and he'd take care of Haskell personally. Haskell took it until the fellow turned away and then slugged him. As usual some of the others broke it up and the boyfriend said if he saw Haskell again he, Haskell, had better be wearing a bulletproof vest."

Fenner got out his leather-covered notebook and an automatic pencil.

"Who's the guy? Is he local?"

"From the Coast. An actor, TV mostly. I think I've seen him once or twice. Supporting parts, works fairly often I gather, but between jobs and came East to be with Miss Moore until this stockholders thing was settled."

"Name?"

"Barry Wilbur. He's staying at the Adams House."

Fenner made a note and said: "All right, I'll talk to her. Now fill me in on Ben Clayton. I take it he's been threatened."

"Only over the phone, anonymously, but he recognized the voice. One threat was overheard by Miss Moore who had stopped by Clayton's apartment and she confirms it."

"Because of this stock thing."

"Plus a more personal matter. Marion Haskell was once Clayton's wife. According to him Haskell is responsible for the divorce—he can give you the details—and she married Haskell on the rebound. Haskell had been married and divorced twice before. So Haskell has not only been chasing around, he's been abusing her. With this stock thing on the fire he'd been holding her a virtual prisoner in the Haskell family home out in Dedham. Somehow—he'll tell you about it—Clayton got her out. Haskell knows it and can't find her. He says he's going to kill Clayton, which in a way is ironic because Haskell and Clayton have been friends—or maybe close companions is a better way of putting it—ever since prep school."

This time Fenner's sigh was audible and again he shook his head.

"I don't know George. You should know I'm not in the bodyguard business."

"I told him that."

"If Haskell is psyched up and temporarily off his rocker it would take an army to protect Clayton and there'd be no guarantee even then. Take Kennedy—"

"Plural, isn't it?"

"No. Those two murders were quite different. The guy that shot the President planned carefully—or someone did—and expected to get away with it. Except for the coincidence of running into that cop in the movie house and then shooting him too he might have made it, at least for a while.

"The nut that killed the Senator did it in front of fifteen or twenty witnesses, knowing he'd be grabbed instantly and possibly killed."

"Okay. Tell Clayton that. But he's got an angle I think you ought to hear. I think it has some merit. The point now is, will you listen?"

"Sure." Fenner tipped one hand and stood up. "You're paying for my time. Why not?"

2

George Tyler's office was furnished in the same general motif as the reception room; utilitarian and designed to impress no one. No more than ten by twelve, it had one window, an ancient and somewhat scarred but well-polished desk, a swivel arm-chair with no padding, and three other straight-backed chairs, none comfortable enough to encourage unnecessary dallying; a green metal filing cabinet.

Nancy Moore was sitting sideways on the chair opposite Tyler's desk, knees crossed, a cigarette between her fingers as she gazed out the window. She straightened when the door opened and took a long and level look at Fenner as the introductions were made.

She nodded but offered no hand as he sat down, the shadowed blue eyes still busy in a guarded way. When she shifted her sights to watch Tyler sit down it was Fenner's turn to appraise and try to classify. In her late twenties, he thought, slender, maybe five four, a yellow raincoat thrown back to reveal a sweater-and-skirt outfit, the skirt knee length but showing some thigh sitting down. The honey-blond hair was pulled back and parted in the middle but instead of a bun on the nape there was a braided effect in the back, fastened there somehow. Good complexion, a rather narrow face, on the bony side, with a pointed chin, hollow cheeks, and a mouth with sensuous implications. He could smell her now, a subtle but effective scent that, while unidentifiable, seemed appropriate.

He had trouble finding a one-word description as Tyler settled himself. There was some sexiness here, an air of worldliness and self-assurance, and something else that took a second more to classify. Intriguing, yes. Exotic, possibly. And now the word came, surprising him because it was seldom associated with a woman her age. Yet it seemed to fit and he accepted it.

The word was decadent.

Tyler, having given them time for mutual inspection, leaned back in his chair and cradled the back of his head in laced fingers.

"I've filled Mr. Fenner in, Nancy, and he agrees it might be a good idea. He thinks he can get a young woman to be with you."

Fenner waited until she looked at him. "What do you think?"

"About what?"

"Will you accept a companion and perhaps take her advice when she feels it's necessary to make suggestions?"

Her shrug was expressive and her reply was both casual and indifferent, the accent slightly throaty.

"Why not? It's no fun going around alone, even without a psycho like Mark Haskell in the picture. I don't like being alone, or eating alone, or going to a movie alone. Can she play gin?"

"If she doesn't you can teach her," Fenner said dryly.

"All right. After all, it's only for five days."

Fenner pulled his chair closer to the desk, indicating the telephone, his brows questioning.

"Sure," Tyler said and pushed the instrument toward him. "Give the number to our operator and she'll get it for you."

Fenner checked the number in his notebook, relayed it. He listened to the dial clicks and the distant ringing. Presently a voice answered and he said: "Mr. Brophy, please, Jack Fenner . . . Ed," he said a moment later. "Could you let me have Kathy Kennedy for the next five or six days? . . . Well, couldn't you take her off that temporarily? I'm calling for an Esterbrook & Warren client from out of town . . . No, no snooping, no tail job; just being a companion to another young woman about her age . . . Okay, hold on."

He found Nancy Moore watching him and said: "Could you meet her for lunch, or at least for a drink?"

"Why not?"

"Lunch would be fine, Ed. Say one o'clock. I'll introduce her," he added and mentioned a small restaurant conveniently located.

He hung up and as Tyler started to replace the telephone it rang. "Yes . . . Oh, yes. Ask him to come to Dave Johnson's office. He's out of town, isn't he? Right."

He stood up. "Ben Clayton," he said and glanced at his watch. "I'd better keep him company until you're ready, Jack. Two offices down the hall." To the girl he said: "You won't need me, Nancy. I imagine Jack will want to ask some questions." He smiled his dignified lawyer's smile. "Be a good girl and answer them, hunh?"

She took out cigarettes and Fenner lit one for her, declining her offer by saying he couldn't get used to filters. When he had his Chesterfield regular going he moved over into Tyler's chair and opened his notebook, aware that she was watching him, the blue eyes speculative and mildly curious.

"No third degree," he said, "but I'd like to clarify certain things. George told me something about your background and your inheritance and why you're in town. I know about the slashed tires and the mugging. You had your handbag with you? And they didn't snatch it, or try to?"

"No. I never even saw them. It was dark. Just down the street from my apartment. There's a low hedge out front and I guess that's where they were waiting. I didn't hear them or if I did it was only an instant before they jumped on my back and I was down. I tried to yell but my face was practically in the sidewalk. They cuffed me on both sides of the head and I got a dandy

punch in the ribs"—she touched lightly an area under the arm-
pit—"and then they left me lying there."

"According to George they said something. What exactly?"

"One said, 'Just a sample, sister. Next time you wind up in the
hospital,' and the other said something like, 'Unless you do what
you're told.'"

"No chance one of them was Haskell?"

"None. I know his voice."

"It wouldn't be too difficult to hire a couple of young punks."

"I know that. But who else but Mark could have coached
them, or wanted them, to say anything about doing what I was
told."

"Meaning give him the proxy for your stock in Haskell &
Company."

"What else?"

Fenner nodded. She was looking out the window now, knees
crossed, the tip of one low-heeled pump tipping up and down
fractionally, as though keeping time to some imagined melody.
When she continued her absent surveillance of the building
across the street he said:

"Tell me about the car thing. I understand it happened on
route one twenty-eight."

"We'd been in Dedham—"

"We meaning you and your boyfriend?"

"His name's Barry Wilbur, or did Mr. Tyler tell you. He's at
the Adams House," she added coolly, "if you want his version."

"Just out for a ride?"

"I wanted to see the house where I lived until my mother
took me away. I didn't remember the street but I asked at a gas
station where the Haskell home was and they knew. All I
remembered was a large white house with high ceilings and
what seemed like an enormous yard out back, and behind that
a stand of trees I used to call my forest."

She went on then to tell what had happened on the way back
and she told it well. The speeding car that cut sharply across the

outside lane; the concrete abutment of the overpass that seemed impossible to miss head on, the tangled mass of shrubbery and vines—she thought it might have been honeysuckle—that cushioned the impact.

She was looking right at him now but there was still distance in her gaze and Fenner listened for inflections and overtones as he had been trained to do in years past. There was, he decided, nothing phoney here. It had happened, at least in her mind, exactly as she said.

"We got out of it," she finished, "with a twisted front bumper and a flattened radiator grill and a small bruise on the forehead for me because I didn't have my belt fastened. And no," she added, forestalling his next question, "neither of us can give you a license number or identify the driver, which is what we told the state policeman who appeared on the scene about five minutes after it happened.

"Barry was too busy braking and hanging onto the wheel to see anything. The one glimpse I had before I covered my face was of a dark sedan, probably newish, and a man with dark glasses and a hat driving. The officer called a tow truck and we phoned for a taxi from the garage. The wreck was a rental job, and the tires had been slashed on the first car, so now it's a taxi or walk."

She twisted in the chair, uncrossing her knees and reaching for another cigarette. When Fenner had supplied a light she thanked him and leaned back, hooking an elbow on a corner of the chair back, the shadowed eyes veiled and watchful.

Fenner met her gaze directly, traces of humor showing at the corners of his mouth, impressed again by her very matter-of-factness and the lack of emotion in her tone and manner.

"I know about your boyfriend's temper. I understand he went looking for Haskell and found him."

"Oh, he has a temper all right. And who could blame him after the accident? He was furious. He said he was going to find Haskell and beat his face in. I argued with him all the way back to town. I thought I'd convinced him. When he told me about it over the phone last night he said he'd threatened Haskell but that it was Haskell who threw the punch when he wasn't looking. He has a gun," she added in the same indifferent cadence, "and he got one for me."

She leaned forward to retrieve her handbag from the corner of the desk. Opening it she gave Fenner a quick look at a small automatic and returned it. He could not identify the make but knew it was foreign, probably Spanish or Italian, and either a .22 or .25.

The unexpected revelation bothered him and he said so. "You have a permit for that?"

"Certainly not."

"It could get you in trouble."

"I'd rather be in trouble than be killed or crippled for life," she said flatly. "I told Barry I'd carry it. I also told him I wouldn't see him again until after the board meeting. He said he'd hang around, and I couldn't stop him, unless I had someone with me whenever I went out. So I said I would. That's why I came to Mr. Tyler."

"He's an actor, Wilbur?"

"And quite a good one."

"Mostly television."

"A few low-budget movies. He hasn't had a lead part yet but he's had some good supporting roles. He does all right, and, who knows, maybe he'll get the right break some day."

"How long have you known him?"

"Maybe three months."

"He came to your shop to get a manicure one day."

For the first time the thin face relaxed and the small laugh and easy smile had much to recommend them.

"A haircut," she said when the laugh bubbled down. "Three times before he asked for a manicure." The smile lingered and her tone was suddenly soft and reminiscent. "The dinner invitation came along with the second manicure, and we decided we liked each other, and—" She let the thought hang and said: "He was married but separated. He'll get the divorce as soon as he and his wife agree on a property settlement."

"Will this be your first?"

"First what?"

"Marriage."

She opened her mouth quickly, brought the lips together, and then the smile—it was more of a smirk really—came again.

"You *are* a nosey bastard, aren't you? . . . No, but why did you sound so sure about it?"

He met the challenge head on and without embarrassment, his eyes amused and knowing now that he liked this girl.

"Because you're too attractive to get by all these years without falling in love once or twice."

"Why thank you, sir," she said dryly and then went on, her tone reverting again, flat and unemotional. "I'd enrolled as a freshman at U.C.L.A. and Lance was a senior. I promised to drop out and marry him when he graduated . . . You see, by then," she said in quick digression, "my stepfather had been killed in a traffic accident. We were never close. He never scolded me or tried to punish me—he left that to mother—but he never showed any affection either. He traveled a lot and quite often—I'd learned to cook pretty early—mother would go with him for two or three days at a time. She'd been a secretary when she finished school here in the East but she thought she was too rusty by then so she spent some money learning how to be a beautician. That's how, later, she got me to learn manicuring."

She was looking out the window again and her mind went quickly back to the main thought.

"Lance was a nut about auto racing and got himself a stock car and then for the next three years we were gypsies. Driving from one track to another, at all hours, and staying in rickety motels and eating steaks when he won a few hundred and hamburg and beans when he didn't. Somehow it didn't seem too bad because we loved each other. Then he spun into a wall, was hit by three other cars, and never regained consciousness."

She stopped abruptly and the silence grew, and because Fenner wanted her to continue the reminiscent mood without thinking too much about it he said:

"Do you remember anything about leaving here with your mother?"

Her eyes came back to him and she thought a moment, an absent frown puckering her arched brows.

"Only that we drove what seemed like a long way. To New York actually and left the car and keys in the airport parking lot and took this plane ride most of the night. Mother had originally come East from the Coast to go to school and she had friends out in California and a couple of cousins. She found a small apartment and a job, and for the first couple of years she'd drop me off at school and one of the cousins would pick me up in the afternoon."

Again the silence came and this time she became aware of it. Looking right at him now, one brow twisting and the eyes sardonic she said:

"Do you really have to know all this just to get me a paid companion for five days? Or maybe you're wondering if I'm an impostor."

"No, not at all." Fenner stood up. "If Esterbrook & Warren checked you out, you're checked out. It's just that I like to get to know the people who employ me. And besides"—he held the yellow raincoat for her—"I get well paid for listening . . . Is it all right if I stop by and see the boyfriend?"

She said of course it was all right and that she would be at the designated restaurant at one.

3

The second office down the hall was an exact duplicate of George Tyler's, and Jack Fenner's glance went first to the man behind the desk. Tyler, on his feet and apparently interrupted in the act of some impatient pacing at the delay, looked relieved as he made the introductions and withdrew, pleading pressures of business.

Ben Clayton stood up and shook hands, and Fenner measured him with a quick appraising glance. Perhaps two inches taller than he was and maybe twenty-five pounds heavier, which would put him at six one, and one ninety-five or better. Thick, prematurely graying hair, metal-rimmed glasses, light-brown eyes that had a vague distracted look in a round placid face.

"Sit down, Jack," he said, at once informal and gesturing. "Sit down . . ."

Fenner sat while Clayton got comfortable behind the desk. Perhaps because of some embarrassment at the prospect of confessing his fears to a stranger, it took him ten seconds to decide on an opening.

"George tells me he filled you in on the rough picture," he said finally. "And you've just talked to Nancy. Did she tell you that she was in my apartment when Mark phoned in one of his threats?"

"She didn't, but George did. That was the third call?"

"Right."

"And I take it you think he means it?"

"I do now. But even if I wasn't sure I'd be a fool not to take some precautions, right?"

Fenner nodded. "And yet you and Haskell have been friends —close companions, George said—since prep school."

"Right again and I think I ought to give you some background so you'll better understand why I have to take Mark seriously. As George says, we met at prep school and that very first time made an impression that remained with me a long time.

"You see I was a high school teacher's son and there on a scholarship, which meant waiting on table and doing odd jobs when requested. Mark had a fat allowance and a sophistication even then that I had to admire. Also, and this is important, I matured late. Thirteen or fourteen before I could detect any signs of pubic hair and I hadn't really started to grow.

"Well, I hadn't been there long when two boys who had been bullying me from time to time caught me alone. They were bigger—a class ahead, and so was Mark at the time—and bouncing me back and forth from one to the other while I tried to keep my feet. Then they started cuffing me and daring me to put up my hands."

He paused, his bespectacled gaze fixed on some image only he could see and softening somehow, as though still touched by the memory.

"I tried," he said finally and shrugged, the eyes refocusing, "more from desperation and outrage than anything else I guess. The next thing I knew my ears were ringing and I was on my back. Then, all of a sudden, I had company. One of the kids was also on the ground and Mark was chasing the other one. Then he stopped and came back, not bothering with the kid who was still on the ground. He picked me up, brushed me off, tucked his arm in mine and said, 'Let's get a hot chocolate,' or something like that. You can imagine what a hero he was to me from then on."

Fenner gave the required nod to show he understood, knowing there was more. Clayton leaned back, a half smile on his
round face, eyes on the molding. That gave Fenner a chance to
study him openly and what he saw confirmed the mental picture that had come to him previously. A figure of conservatism,
Clayton wore a dark-blue suit, three-button, complete with
vest; the only thing missing was an old-fashioned watch chain
draped across the folds. A white shirt with French cuffs, a plain
navy tie.

Now, his glance still fixed upward, Clayton said: "I discovered
much later that there was an odd ambivalence in Mark's character. I don't mean the usual love-hate thing, though there could
have been some of that between Mark and his father, Mark
never quite measuring up and getting little if any love or affection, assuming the old man was capable of such emotions, which
I doubt. No, what I mean is there seemed to be two forces
battling each other inside him. He could be, and often was,
generous with his money and possessions, protective, at least
when we were young, at times considerate and understanding.
Yet there was an ingrown mean streak too, some wish for vengeance when he felt slighted or hurt, and no capacity for compassion or forgiveness when the mood was there."

"A guy who'd hold a grudge," Fenner said to help keep the
confession going.

"Exactly. When I began to get my growth he gave me his
cast-off clothes which were practically new and far better than
anything I could afford. He took me home with him for part of
my first Christmas holiday and asked me to spend two weeks of
summer vacation at their place on Cape Cod."

He sighed, lips twisting. "Of course what I was actually, was
his toady. He wanted a flunky and his father helped. He took
a liking to me, sort of took me into the family. Later he told me
I was a steadying influence on Mark and went out of his way to
show his appreciation. I felt an obligation by then, a rather
weighty one as it turned out. Without realizing it I became a

young paid companion. To show you what I mean, consider my education.

"Mark and I finished prep school together and went on to Cornell. They bounced him during his sophomore year, and he came back in the fall. When he was busted again he managed to transfer to Virginia and the old man said if I'd transfer with him he'd take care of the tuition, board, and room for me. Because that meant no more waiting on table in the fraternity, no odd jobs, I thought, why the hell not?"

He went on to tell how he'd been offered a job in the family business after graduation and as he elaborated Fenner got as comfortable as possible in an uncomfortable chair, shoulder blades on the chair back, edge of buttocks on the seat, legs outthrust, and ankles crossed. In his gray slacks, blue flannel jacket, and button-down shirt with a red-and-blue-striped tie, he looked about as much like the popular conception of a private investigator as a space salesman for a national magazine. Only the inquisitive and appraising look in the direct green eyes suggested he might be experienced in the intricacies of the criminal mind.

Now, rousing himself, he said: "I think I've got the picture. When did the psycho in him start to show?"

Clayton spread his hands, thought a moment, pushed back from the desk and stood up. The strain, the signs of tension in the placid face were beginning to show and he stepped over to the window, speaking with his back to the room.

"So you'll understand, I'll have to talk about girls for a moment. I had two in college at various times and he took both of them away from me. With one he just sort of broke up when he'd made his conquest; the other left school, pregnant some said, with the old man's money paying her off. He'd been married twice before Marion, and in each case the wife was so relieved to get rid of him she settled for a modest lump sum, again supplied by the old man. I should have told you that Mark had very little of his own.

"Well, during his second marriage I fell in love. Her name was Marion Lawrence. Good family and reasonably well off—her father was a doctor and they lived in Hingham. She was so much better than anything Mark had been able to get that he tried to move in. For once the natural charm and sophistication and easy manners weren't quite enough. Anyway she married me. We had to get together socially now and then, and she liked him well enough—perhaps she was just amused by his efforts—but he was so obvious that she simply accepted him in a tolerant sort of way. Until one night she caught me out of school, the one and only time I was ever out of line. I found out later that the son of a bitch set me up so she'd find me bare-assed with some hundred-dollar-date girl."

The phrase, so bluntly, almost viciously, put, sounded strange coming from so quiet a man, and when he wheeled from the window the anger and resentment showed.

"I don't want to go into it," he said, thin-lipped now and emphatic. "Just take my word that from then on I made up my mind to get even with him, and now I've got some help. For one thing, Marion knows it was a mistake to marry him. I'm sure she'll remarry me. She already has put a private investigator—I don't know his name—to work gathering divorce evidence, which she now has. Then Nancy Moore was located within the time limit the old man set, and as the daughter, the codicil gave her shares of company stock equal to those Mark inherited.

"He knows I'm the one who instigated the talks with Allied General and brought them to a head. If he can't vote Nancy's shares, and he's not going to get them, he can't block the takeover unless he can swing some of the smaller holders . . . Did George tell you anything about the present distribution?"

"He broke it all the way for me."

"Good. Then you can understand that Mark's probably been working on some of them to influence them to vote his way. With Marion's ten percent plus his twenty-four he might have an outside chance. Without them he's dead. But he can't vote them if he can't find her, and if she shows up at the meeting she'll vote my way.

"The guy has flipped," he added flatly. "You know, or I assume you do, what he's been trying to do to Nancy Moore. To get Marion's proxy he began to abuse her physically. For a few days he actually held her prisoner in the family home so she couldn't countermand the proxy she'd been forced to sign. He hired some tough Amazon to keep her locked up. Until I figured a way to get her out of there the other day. A friend of mine who's in Europe gave me the key to his flat and that's where she is now."

Fenner pulled in his legs, sat up, and reached for cigarettes. The one small ashtray on the desk was clean but Clayton saw the look and produced a leather case. When he had a cigarette of his own he spun flame from a silver Zippo and offered it at arm's length.

"The wife," Fenner said when he had a light. "Can I have the address? Is it all right if I go see her and hear her side of it?"

The questions narrowed the light-brown eyes and some new suspicion showed.

"Are you going to work for me? What I'm telling you is confidential?"

Fenner said, "Absolutely. At least the confidential part. If you can pay the freight I'll work for you." When he had made a note of the address he said: "You're convinced that Haskell's threats are not just talk?"

"You're damn right I am."

"You think he's psycho enough, temporarily anyway, to walk up to you in a crowd and start shooting?"

"No. I think we can rule that out. With his ego I think he expects to get away with it, one way or another."

"Do you think he'd have the sort of contacts that would put him in touch with a pro?"

"Possibly, but I doubt it. The way he is now I really think he'd rather take his chance and maybe risk a trial than let me sell the company out from under him and take his wife away." He shook his head, tight-lipped and determined. "No. He'll either try it himself or not at all."

"Okay," Fenner said evenly, convinced now and understanding the problem. "But as I told George Tyler there's no guarantee that I can have you protected under all circumstances."

"I'm aware of that. I assume you'll have help?"

"What I think I need. But even so—"

This time Clayton cut in. "I'm not talking about protection. That's not why I'm hiring you."

Few things made Jack Fenner blink but now he did, his surprise showing.

"Oh?"

"My idea," Clayton said, measuring his words, "is a bit different. See what you think of it. Okay?"

"Okay."

"What I want you to do is *watch Haskell, not me.* If you can keep an eye on him—is tail the proper word?—you'll be in a position to tip me off, won't you? Someone should be able to block any attempt on me, assuming he should make one. If he gets close, I mean outside the office, one of your men will be around, right?"

Fenner took time to put out his cigarette and was suddenly aware that he was impressed. The idea, while not perfect—and what idea was?—had merit. So intent was he on the possibilities that he missed the next few words.

"Sorry," he said. "I was thinking."

"I said, can you do it?"

"Sure."

"Fine. Then I guess that's it."

"Not quite," Fenner said, and grinned. "If you've seen some private investigators on television you may remember money is seldom mentioned. The hero takes a case because someone, often a friend or acquaintance, is in trouble and needs help. You assume, I suppose, that the client can afford it and maybe sometime he'll pay, or maybe it's just for old time's sake. In real life it's a bit different. We have to make a living, hopefully a very nice one."

Clayton's eyes opened at the announcement and then he chuckled, waving aside the problem.

"Sure. Naturally. I understand. But hell, it's only for five days. I don't care if it costs me two thousand bucks."

"And it very well could."

That got him. He sat down again. He swallowed once, his mouth slightly agape and the light-brown eyes wide. Then he put his face back together.

"Really. As much as that? How many men do you plan on using?"

"I have two in mind at the moment."

"And may I ask how and what you charge?"

"By the hour. For me twenty dollars. The others get eight but they'll be working a lot more hours than I will. I also ought to point out, in case the thought hasn't occurred to you, that being around for that board meeting doesn't necessarily mean you'll be in the clear."

This time a frown came and Clayton seemed to be having trouble assimilating the suggestion.

"You mean that even when Haskell's out he might still try to kill me?"

"It's possible, isn't it? If the guy wants revenge, and from what you say he might, his motive, having lost his wife *and* his job, is still there, isn't it?"

Again Clayton thought awhile and finally, surprisingly, a slow smile came, adding some new attractiveness to his face. He shook his head, the smile constant.

"No. I've known him too long. You lick him once, and good, and he stays licked. I told you he was my protector for a couple of years. By college I was bigger. I could always lick him. I only had to twice. After that he'd back off. No. If there is an attempt now or later, he'll do it himself. And anyway," he added cheerfully, "if I can bring off the takeover and get Marion back I'll take my chances."

Fenner nodded. He stretched, flexing his shoulder blades, and came to his feet, amused glints in his eyes and aware that he was beginning to like this man.

"One thing more, two things actually, the first a matter of curiosity. How much money is involved? How much are the shares going to bring, I mean the value in the Allied General stock you'll get in exchange."

"Fifteen million, roughly. The tax situation will be a factor."

"Fifteen million for the plant, machinery, inventories, good will?"

Clayton came round the desk, his smile widening. "We were never one of the big boys. And you've heard of short-term bank loans? And long-term loans that insurance companies make on the proper collateral? Allied assumes our indebtedness. The fifteen is net to the shareholders before taxes."

"Oh," said Fenner inadequately, chagrined by his ignorance. "Then your five percent would be worth seven-fifty and Mrs. Haskell's a million and a half."

"Right."

"The other thing," Fenner said as they started for the door. "I'd like to see Haskell for a few minutes close up."

"Why not? Our city office is just around the corner."

"So how do I get in? Suppose he refuses to see me."

"Hah!" Clayton said with some glee. "You'll get in all right because I'll take you in personally. I generally hold forth at our main office in Weymouth but I have a small cubby next to Haskell's office I use when I'm in the city . . . Sure," he added, still pleased as he opened the door. "I'll introduce you and you can take it from there, okay?"

"Good enough. But there's one thing more I'd like to get from you. Try to find out from Haskell's secretary or someone what his plans are for the afternoon. Appointments if any, what time he is expected to leave the office. When you have some sort of line on him phone my office and leave word with my secretary . . . Also," he put his hand on Clayton's arm to keep him out of the hall, "I'll need a photo. One that I can have copied."

Clayton stood there a moment frowning and then his face brightened. "There's a good one in our last annual report. I'll get our receptionist in the office to dig up a couple or three copies."

As they started down the hall Fenner was aware that the vague distracted look that had been stamped on Clayton's face when he had first entered the office had been replaced by one of confidence and satisfaction.

4

The local offices of Haskell & Company were indeed just around the corner, the building somewhat smaller but newer-looking than the one they had just left. The suite was on the fourth floor and Clayton ushered Fenner into a modern reception room with indirect lighting, tastefully done in modern but comfortable-looking furniture, the carpet twice as thick as the one at Esterbrook & Warren. Here there was no old-fashioned glassed-in cage but a flat-topped desk presided over by a nice appearing gray-haired woman in a brown business suit. Covering the back of a book she had been reading with some papers as she glanced up, she smiled at Clayton and gave Fenner a quick inspection, as though assessing his status and potentiality.

Making no introduction, Clayton said: "Do you think you could dig up three or four copies of our last annual report, Madge?"

"Certainly, Mr. Clayton. Right away."

"Mr. Fenner will pick them up on his way out if you'll have them ready. I don't imagine he'll be too long."

As he turned away he winked at Fenner and jerked his chin toward the corridor on his left. In back of the partition that isolated the reception room was a glassed-in area above the chest-high wall where two men and three girls were either bent over desks or operating business machines. Beyond this, as Clayton continued down the short hall, were three doors, one on each side and one at the end.

"My city domain," Clayton said, not glancing backward but flipping a thumb at the right hand door; then he was opening the last one and standing aside to wave Fenner ahead of him.

This office, unlike George Tyler's, might have been acceptable as a television background for a successful business executive. The maroon carpet was thick and immaculate, the walls paneled but bare, and there were two windows. The divan and three matching chairs in dark leather looked expensive and in one corner was a bar, open for business on top with a small refrigerator beneath. The massive desk diagonally placed near one corner held an intercom and two telephones, one of which was being used by the man who glanced up in annoyance, frowned, and kept talking.

Clayton said: "You want a drink?" and gestured.

Fenner shook his head and stopped a few feet in front of the desk, the green eyes busy in his angular impassive face, evaluating this man he had seen from time to time but never at close range.

About Clayton's age, he thought, before he recalled that this was true. Probably his own height but stockier, casually correct in the cashmere jacket, the slacks hidden from view. Medium-brown hair, stylishly long. The bony brow made the pale-blue eyes seem hooded, and together with the close-set ears gave him somehow the appearance of a compassionless satyr. Those eyes were watching him now as Haskell continued to talk and Fenner's mind went back, associating that particular shade of blue with certain criminal types he had arrested and questioned. Almost always these individuals were associated with some form of violence and he had found most of them cruel, ruthless, and quite devoid of conscience. Recalling all this he was about ready to accept Ben Clayton's assessment: this man could kill remorselessly given the right sort of provocation.

None of this showed now as Haskell hung up and turned to Clayton, his tone irritable but politely so.

"What the hell is this, Ben? You could at least knock." The glance shifted to Fenner again. "Who's your friend?"

"Jack Fenner."

"Representing what company?"

"No company, Mark. A private investigator. Recommended by Esterbrook & Warren."

"Oh. Hired by whom?"

"Me and Nancy Moore."

Haskell started to speak, his irritation mounting. He took time to disguise it and tried again.

"Do you mind telling me why?"

"Because I'm getting fed up with your telephone threats— and on the last one I have a witness—and Nancy is getting annoyed with the various methods of harassment you arranged, hoping to scare her into giving you her proxy."

Haskell's grin had become fixed and contemptuous. "You're hallucinating, Ben. Is that all you wanted?"

"For me, yes. Whatever Mr. Fenner wants he can speak for himself. He asked to meet you, and having made the introduction I'll move on to my office."

He grinned at Fenner, gave Haskell a small bow that was open mockery and went out.

"All right." Haskell leaned back in his leather-backed executive's chair, placed his hands carefully on the arms. "I still don't know what Ben's talking about," he said, his tone openly derisive, "but if either he or Miss Moore had any evidence to substantiate his insinuations he'd go to the police or the district attorney, right?"

"Right."

"So what do *you* want?"

"Just to get a close look at you. I like to know who I'm working on."

"Working on?" His expression seemed to indicate genuine

amazement as he let the spring of the chair snap him upright. "What the hell is that supposed to mean?"

"We want to be sure you behave yourself and I thought you ought to know we'll"—his ambiguousness was deliberate—"be keeping an eye on things, at least until next Monday."

"Get out, Fenner!" The words were clipped and furious. "Or get thrown out!"

Fenner had moved close to the desk, his tight smile fixed and his gaze watchful, unable to remember when he had taken such a dislike to a man in so short a time.

"Not by you, Mr. Haskell. You're going to need a bit of help. After all, I was invited here, remember?"

Unable any longer to contain his anger, Haskell grabbed the telephone. As he lifted the handset Fenner reached forward and depressed the activating bar, cutting the connection. He was ready in case Haskell slammed the handset on his hand, and watched the beginning of just such a move. Then the lifted hand stopped in midair, hanging suspended. After a second or two Fenner removed the finger. Haskell then replaced the handset in a normal way and now the mean grin came as he acknowledged the checkmate.

"Threats," he said with quiet sarcasm. "I'm the one who got threatened. Yesterday afternoon. In the University Club bar. You can check it out."

Fenner moved back. "I heard about it. One of your famous sneak punches when the other guy isn't looking."

"He threatened to kill me. I have witnesses. You want to keep an eye on things? Then maybe you'd better turn your attention to a would-be actor named Barry Wilbur. Now if you don't mind—"

Apparently giving up further thoughts of attempted force, he picked up a thin stack of correspondence, pressed the intercom and said: "Will you come in please, Miss Cantrell, and bring your notebook." He was smiling now as he continued to Fenner.

"Just a bit of correspondence that needs my attention. Sit down. Make yourself comfortable."

This time Fenner eyed the other with some amusement, admiring the sudden switch in attitude and giving Haskell credit for handling the situation in a manner that left him little choice but to withdraw quietly. As he turned away he met Miss Cantrell coming in.

Coming out of the building, Jack Fenner swung left and started briskly up the street. The day was clear and sunny but there was still some bite in the air and for a moment he wished he had brought his topcoat. He moved easily, threading his way through the sidewalk traffic, eyes straight ahead as he planned his itinerary.

He had arrived at Esterbrook & Warren by taxi and he was pleased that he could cover the rest of his travels on foot. It was only a few blocks to the Adams House, a few more to Armandos to introduce Kathy Kennedy to Nancy Moore, and even a shorter distance from there to his office. He thought briefly of stopping by a telephone booth to find if Barry Wilbur was in but by the time he found one the hotel was only a block and a half away so he kept moving.

Getting the room number from the desk clerk, he went to the house telephones. When a man's voice answered the second ring he identified himself, said he had been talking to Nancy Moore and was it all right to come up.

The man who opened the door of six eighteen was younger than he was, maybe in his late twenties he thought, and fitted very well the image of a television actor. A bit more than average height, he had a lithe, well-muscled body, and a confident easy way of moving. Dark hair, far too shaggy for Fenner's taste, and dark eyes with thick brows that nearly met over the bridge of his nose. The swart coloring and facial structure suggested some foreign ancestry and made him wonder whether the name was genuine or had been adopted for professional purposes. His dress was appropriate, the red slacks tight-fitting, the wild colorful shirt unbuttoned nearly to the navel. But the smile was genuine, the greeting hearty.

"Hi," he said. "Come in. I was just having a pre-luncheon snort." He indicated the half-filled glass in his hand. "How about joining me?"

Fenner smiled back at him as he entered and waited for the door to close, noting the accent which, while rough and the words vernacular, suggested some dramatic training. He felt the hand on his arm drawing him politely toward the tray with its bowl of ice, soda, good Scotch, and an empty glass.

"All right, thanks," he said. "I have a luncheon date so it will have to be a light one."

"Good. Why don't you pour your own."

He waited until Fenner had his drink and waved him to the one comfortable chair in the room which stood by the lone window and a floor lamp.

"Nancy phoned me after she'd talked to you. She liked you . . . And I guess she's right," he added not waiting for a response. "I mean about having an experienced girl dick with her the next few days. I was against it at first. You know, like it was a reflection on my not being able to take care of her myself. I guess she told you I'm a bit of a hothead," he said and grinned, the perfect teeth, whether capped or natural, gleaming whitely.

"She did mention it," Fenner said, with some amusement and his gaze reflective as he continued his unobtrusive inspection. "She also said you got yourself in a hassle at the University Club."

"Yeah!" A pause and then the tone hardened. "But if you'd been with us yesterday morning when that car deliberately tried to force us into that abutment you might have felt the same way. I'd have killed the bastard on the spot if I could have got my hands on him.

"I was still steaming when we got back to town, and the more I thought of it the hotter I got. If you could just have been there," he said again. "I couldn't eat lunch; too worked up. Because there couldn't be any question about who did it, or was behind it, after what had happened to Nancy before. So after I took her home I tried to get a line on Haskell. I got nowhere with his secretary. He was out for the afternoon, she said. But I knew about Ben Clayton and he finally told me where the guy might be later in the afternoon.

"I didn't have any trouble getting into the University Club, said I had an appointment with Haskell. He was in the bar with five or six other guys, drinking it up and laughing when I went up to him. I told him who I was, ready to slug him but willing to give him the first swing so I could really lay it on him . . . The son of a bitch never opened his mouth. Just listened, staring with those fishy eyes of his and that mean smirk on his mouth. I didn't raise my voice, didn't attract any attention, didn't want to."

"What did you tell him?"

"I don't remember all of it, something about I knew what he'd been doing to Nancy and why. When I'd finished telling about the accident that damn near killed the both of us, I called him a few names and said if he, or anybody, laid a finger on Nancy again I was going to look him up and beat his brains out.

"I don't know why I didn't do it then." He grunted softly, a bitter sound. "All he did was sort of half nod, and when I knew he had the message and wasn't going to swing I made a mistake. I was more disgusted than angry by then, and instead of backing away like I should have with a tricky bastard like that I started to turn and he unloaded."

He touched the side of his jaw, his expression rueful and chagrined. "Right here," he said. "Pow! Didn't hurt, didn't even stun me but my feet got tangled and I went down hard. I rolled over, knowing I really was going to kill him, and four guys grabbed me. When I saw I couldn't break away, and not wanting a brawl, I relaxed."

"You threatened him then, in front of witnesses, right?"

"I sure did. And right then I meant every word of it. I said

I was going to kill him and that if I ever ran into him again he'd better be wearing a bulletproof vest . . . Somebody asked me if I was a member and I said no and the four of them hustled me to the elevator and waited till the door closed."

That was a lot of talk and he let his breath out slowly, looked distastefully at his empty glass, started to get up, and then changed his mind. After he had put the glass on the floor beside his chair he looked up and grinned broadly.

"I guess I blew it, hunh?"

Fenner returned the grin. He couldn't help it. Such simple honesty, the sheer audacity of Wilbur's one attempt at vengeance overcame the latent suspicion that this could be a potential killer.

"How do you feel about it now?"

"I'd still like to beat his face in. And I will if he bothers Nancy again. I guess I'm smart enough to know killing is something else."

"But you do have a gun."

The remark wiped out the lingering, embarrassed smile. The dark eyes narrowed and the facial muscles hardened as the lips compressed.

"Nancy told you, hunh?"

"She also showed me one you'd given her."

"So what?" The truculence was showing now. "You going to turn us in to the law?"

"Not unless you use it."

"If I do no one will ever find it."

"Do you have a permit, either of you?"

"I do. In California."

"Bring the guns with you?"

"No. I didn't know we'd be dealing with a psycho. You can pick up a piece anywhere if you drift around and can pay for it."

Fenner was aware that what Wilbur said was true; he had also begun to wonder if there wasn't just a touch of psycho in the actor in his present mood. Before he could dwell on the thought Wilbur said:

"This chick that's going to be with Nancy. Competent, is she? Dependable?"

"I think so."

"Not just some watchdog dame that looks like a dick?"

"I think the two will get along fine."

He watched Wilbur lean over to pick up his glass. He strode to the tray, poured generously. When he'd added an ice cube and some water he took a large swallow and remembered his manners.

"You?" he said, mood changing and his actor's smile taking over to show he'd forgiven the questioning. "Want to lunch?"

Fenner stood up and moved over to put his empty glass on the tray. He said he had a date.

"With your girl and mine. I want to introduce them and see how they get along." He shook hands, noting the strong-fingered grip. At the door he turned back. "A bit of gratuitous advice. It's going to be kind of boring for you the next few days. Why don't you fly to the Coast and then come back Sunday or Monday? That way you won't need the gun."

Wilbur shook his head. "I'd rather stick around. You know, just in case."

"Suit yourself. Just leave the gun here when you go out, okay?"

Wilbur nodded and now there was an undertone of good humor in his reply.

"I'll consider your suggestion with due care." . . .

Downstairs Fenner found the public telephones just off the lobby and closed himself in one of the booths. With his notebook out he told the operator he wanted to make a credit-card call to Los Angeles. When he had given her the proper number he glanced at his watch. Nine-thirty Pacific time, which should be about right to catch Bart Johnson before he went out. He had never met the man personally but he had corresponded with him and twice used him, the last time about a year ago. Once he had been asked by Johnson to locate a witness supposed to be living in the city.

"Bart," he said when a man's voice finally answered. "Jack Fenner. Of the East Coast Fenners."

"Hey, Jackson." The hearty response came at once. "How you doin'?"

"Some good days, some bad."

"Ain't it the truth."

"I've got a small job for you. It shouldn't take too much of your time."

"I can probably squeeze it in. Shoot."

"Two names. Got a pencil? . . . Barry Wilbur. An actor. The name could be phoney but it's the one he'd be using. He works at it so he'd be registered with Central Casting, the Screen Actors Guild, the TV Actors Guild if there is such a thing. Get what you can for maybe the last two or three years. He's got a girl named Nancy Moore. Concentrate on him—he's a hothead and could have a rap sheet—but it shouldn't be too hard to see what's with her. Supposed to work in a Beverly Hills barber shop and I don't imagine there are many of those in a ritzy town like that."

"Hah!" said Johnson. "How right you are. No barber shops. Two tonsorial parlors. Hair styling for men twenty-five bucks; a plain haircut seven-fifty."

"Good enough. Call you back the same time tomorrow and if I can't make it I'll try again at noon your time, okay?"

"I'll have something for you."

"And bill me at your number-one rate because I've got a couple of clients who can afford it."

Referring again to his notebook without leaving the booth, he spent the next five minutes making local calls. It took that long to line up two men who could help him with the job.

5

Armandos was a smallish, low-ceilinged, intimate, almost tea-roomy restaurant that some might call cute. The food was quite good but the size of the portions did not appeal to hearty eaters. Fenner, having selected it because there was small chance of him running into anyone he knew, arrived five minutes early. The hatcheck girl looked disappointed when she saw there was no hat or coat but managed a small smile as he eased down on the black settee in the outer alcove.

Kathy Kennedy was only about a minute behind him, and this pleased him because he had counted on her being early. She was wearing a wool business suit with a white blouse, a sturdy, fresh-faced girl with a firm-fleshed body and an abundance of freckles. The Irish blue eyes, contrasting attractively with her black hair, had a direct and interested way of looking at you and her handclasp was firm as she said:

"Hello, Mr. Fenner."

"Mister," said Fenner with wry good humor. "That's what happens when you get old; all the good-looking girls mister you."

She smiled to show she appreciated the compliment and said: "They told me always to be respectful to a client."

Fenner said okay and led her to the settee. As he began to fill her in about Nancy Moore he recalled the things he knew about Kathy. That she had wanted to be at least indirectly associated with the detective world until she was ready for marriage was understandable enough, considering her heritage. Father, brother, brother-in-law—all were police officers of varying grades; even her current boyfriend was a precinct plainclothes-man. That she had not followed the official line was due to a certain feminine independence that, she was smart enough to realize, was not always appreciated in the police hierarchy. With her connections it was a simple matter to find a spot with a small agency whose business was confined for the most part to a two-or-three state operation. By now she'd had a year of experience and the more he talked to her and listened to her replies the more convinced he was that he had made the proper choice for this particular assignment.

Nancy Moore was only a few minutes late and Fenner had about finished with Kathy. Now she smiled at them as they stood up, her eyes very busy indeed as they made their quick overall inspection and Fenner realized at once how very differ-ent the two women were.

Both were attractive, but Kathy's fresh, open-faced prettiness contrasted sharply with the somewhat brittle worldliness of the older woman and he remembered again the word that had come to him back in George Tyler's office. He saw no reason now to revise his opinion and, taking each girl lightly by the arm, he steered them past the cozy bar into the main room and the table he had reserved.

When they were seated he said: "I'm sorry I can't buy you lunch. Not that it matters much." He glanced at Nancy with one eye and then with both. "Since I'd probably put the tab on my expense account anyway. But I can buy a drink while you two get acquainted . . . What will it be?" he added when the waiter approached.

Nancy showed no hesitation. "A very dry martini with a twist, straight up" . . . "I think—maybe a Cinzano and soda, with a bit of orange peel," Kathy said, and Fenner asked for a Scotch and water.

When the waiter withdrew he took one of the Haskell & Company annual reports from his side pocket. It was not an elaborate production and he assumed that, since there were so few stockholders, it was printed and distributed for mailing to customers and prospective customers to show the soundness of its financial position. When he came to the halftone of Mark Haskell he folded the page back and handed it to Kathy.

"He's the one that's been making the threats."

She studied it a moment before she glanced up. "He's rather attractive, isn't he? He doesn't look like the violent type—except maybe for the eyes."

"He's a bit more than violent now," Nancy said flatly. "The man is headed straight for the psychiatric ward if you want my opinion."

Kathy continued to study the photograph for another few seconds and then, looking right at Fenner, she asked the question that he knew would come up and had heretofore avoided mentioning.

"Am I to keep my gun with me?"

Fenner still wasn't sure and he said so. "I don't know, Kathy."

Nancy had no such reservations. "I *know* she should."

"Have you ever used it?" Fenner asked.

"They say I'm quite good on the pistol range but"—Kathy hesitated, her small smile shy—"no. I never shot at anyone. I only had to show it twice. It helped at the time."

"Do you have it in your bag now?"

"Yes, but I can always drop it off at the office, or home, if you think I should. I've had some karate and I know two or three good judo chops."

Nancy had other ideas and she stated them, her red mouth tight and determined.

"No. Definitely. She keeps hers and I keep mine," she added and tapped her own bag for emphasis.

The stubborn set of the chin and the bleak look told Fenner

it was pointless to argue. Kathy carried the gun or he would be told to get someone else, and just how was he to get someone as good on short notice?

"All right, all right," he said and was glad the waiter appeared with the drinks. When they had been served he said, "Cheers," as pleasantly as he could and held his glass up until they replied.

"I talked with Barry Wilbur," he said to get off the subject. "He has a bit of a low boiling point himself, hasn't he?"

"That's why I'm not going to see him. That business at the University Club was just too much."

"I made a suggestion. He didn't buy it."

"What suggestion?"

"That he fly to the Coast and fly back after the board meeting to pick you up."

"He doesn't care much for suggestions unless they are his own. So let him sit and play solitaire if that's what he wants." She turned to Kathy and changed the subject abruptly, as though to cleanse her mind of all thoughts of Barry Wilbur and his problems. "I'm renting a drab three-room furnished apartment temporarily. There is really no extra sleeping room—the sofa has its own built-in discomfort—so you won't have to spend the night. Anyway there's a double lock on the door."

Kathy said she understood. "Mr. Fenner told me I was to come to your place whenever you wanted me to in the morning—"

"Yes," said Nancy interrupting. "And don't eat breakfast, I mean nothing more than a cup of coffee. I like to fix breakfast and I don't like to eat alone."

"—and I'm to stay with you as long as you want in the evenings," Kathy finished as though there had been no interruption.

"Miss Moore asked me if you played gin," Fenner said.

"Oh, yes," Kathy said. "And chess and even checkers sometimes when my grandfather stops in."

"We'll take in some movies and maybe a matinee if there are any shows trying out in town, maybe go to the track one day,"

Nancy added, showing for the first time some enthusiasm about the coming association and a genuine liking for Kathy Kennedy.

Fenner took a breath, let it out with some relief, and beckoned for the drink check. He put a five on the tray, which left an adequate tip, excused himself and stood. He said he was sorry he could not eat with them and touched Kathy lightly on the shoulder.

"If anything comes up that you're doubtful about, call me. If I'm not at the office the answering service will know where to find me."

He glanced at Nancy and found her shadowed eyes veiled and reflective. He met her gaze soberly and spoke quietly.

"I think you two will get along fine."

"I do too, and thanks for arranging it."

"Just listen to her, please, if she has a suggestion from time to time." He winked at Kathy and turned, not giving Nancy a chance to reply.

Jack Fenner had his office in a smallish, four-storied building just around the corner from Boylston, a somewhat ancient structure that had been made more presentable by sandblasting the façade and modernizing the interior. The foyer had been neatly redone and an automatic elevator replaced the creaking grilled cage.

The pebbled glass in the upper half of the door on the left side of the third-floor corridor bore only one name: J. H. FENNER, with no hint of his occupation. There had once been another name below this, a none too successful middle-aged lawyer who had been killed more than a year ago. The extra room of the suite that could be entered from here or, more directly from the next door down the hall, was temporarily occupied by a young C.P.A. trying to make it on his own. In terms of class and yearly rental it was several notches above Fenner's original one-room headquarters, all he could afford when he first started on his own.

The walls of the anteroom were paneled in real wood, though a veneer; there was a good green carpet, an imitation leather chair, and four others with seats of matching material. A black coffee table held reasonably current copies of *Life, Sports Illustrated,* and *Newsweek;* there were plenty of ashtrays and two drum lamps on the end tables.

When Fenner came in after a sandwich-and-beer lunch, Alice Maxwell was at her desk behind a waist-high partition in one corner and as he saw her quick and ready smile he realized again how much he would miss her when she married her young man, who was in his last year of internship at the medical school. She held up two telephone messages and said:

"Mr. Kinlaw and Mr. Valano are already here. I told them it was all right if they waited in your office."

The inner door stood open and he went on to his private office, which was done much like the anteroom with the addition of a fireproof metal filing cabinet and a well-filled bookcase. Jake Kinlaw was sitting in his, Fenner's, chair, Tom Valano at one side, and Kinlaw came out of the chair mumbling something about wanting to see what it felt like to sit in a desk chair like that.

Fenner nodded and said hello, impressed again by the startling difference in the two men. Kinlaw, a veteran police officer who had been retired ten years or so had his hat on. He seemed always to have a hat on because he had an expanding U-shaped bald area extending from his forehead to the crown. Young Valano probably did not own a hat, and his thick hair was worn long but not quite long enough to attract attention, the beard neatly trimmed which made him look more like a graduate student than a private investigator—he was not yet licensed but had his application in. An ex–combat photographer, he was a camera bug and his value came from his ability to get photos without the subjects knowing their pictures had been taken.

Fenner continued his mental evaluation as he went behind the desk, moved the correspondence tray one inch to one side, pushed the stand holding a portable electric typewriter two inches closer to the desk.

Kinlaw, a beefy man and none too neat, had been allowed to resign from the force after twenty years rather than face an inquiry into some matter involving several other officers thought to be doing minor favors for certain gamblers. To augment his half-pension he had done security work for a while, had a stint with a larger agency, and now was available to do free-lance work, sharing office space and an answering service with three other freelancers, not all in investigating work. Valano, tall, lanky, and brash, had worked for Kent Murdock on the *Courier* for a while but the routine bored him. He sold a spot-news photo from time to time but seemed content to shoot away with his various cameras in an investigative capacity.

Before Fenner sat down he gave each of them a copy of the Haskell annual report and told them to look at the photograph on the first inside page. Kinlaw nodded.

"Name of Haskell, right?"

"Right."

"I've seen him around."

"You, Tom?"

Valano frowned and shook his head. "I don't think so. Is he the one we're interested in?"

Fenner said yes and gave them a brief résumé of the things Ben Clayton had told him. "I'm in on it through the law firm of Esterbrook & Warren."

"And this Clayton," Kinlaw said, "really thinks that Haskell may try to knock him off."

"Enough so to pay us to prevent it."

"Well the idea isn't too bad," Kinlaw said. "I mean to watch this Haskell instead of trying to protect Clayton. How do you want to work it?"

Fenner glanced at his watch. "Clayton's supposed to give me a ring and let me know when Haskell is likely to leave his office . . . Write this down," he said and gave them the State Street address. "Also this," he added and mentioned the address of Haskell's apartment. "He has a home in Dedham but he's using the apartment now, according to Clayton. I know the building, a converted brownstone, three floors, and my guess is it probably has been cut into six apartments, three to a floor. If Clayton doesn't phone before you're ready to leave I'll call him.

"You," he glanced at Valano, "pick up Haskell and stay with him until he comes home. You, Jake, find the super or janitor for the building. There's a larger apartment house next door and there's a good chance he's taking care of both buildings. Find out who the tenants are. Tell him you're taking a city census or whatever you think will work—"

"Can I grease him if I have to?"

Fenner grinned and said: "Just so you don't get too generous with the client's dough . . . And when you have what you want —I mean names, occupations, anything else that might be pertinent—you're off until after your dinner, and don't eat too late. Be back at the apartment, parked where you can see the entrance, at say, seven-thirty. If Haskell is already there, Tom will be outside; if not wait till Tom shows and then take it from there."

"Until when?"

"Use your own judgment." Fenner leaned forward, hands at ease on the desk top, the green eyes full of thought. "If he's already inside I'd hang around until maybe one or one-thirty; he probably won't be going anywhere at that hour. If he comes in, well, the same thing I guess. What we want to know is who else comes in while you're on, and at what time."

Valano shifted in his chair and crossed his bony knees, one foot dangling. "Is it okay to make a suggestion? . . . What I mean is, Jake's a hell of a lot more experienced than I am on a tail job. If I could work nights I'd like to experiment with a new fast film that will catch most things with no more than the available light, like a street lamp. No flash to tip anyone off."

This time Fenner's glance held a suggestion of respect.

"You've got a point." He thought a while. Jake Kinlaw was like a bulldog and his appearance, even his size was so nondescript as to be almost unnoticeable except to an extremely suspicious subject. Young Valano with his beard and casual dress—he'd wear a tie and jacket only when instructed to do so—would never be taken for an investigator; on the other hand, once noticed he'd be remembered.

"Let's switch tomorrow," Fenner said finally. "Both of you," he added, "be there at seven-thirty in the morning. When Haskell leaves for the office you take over, Jake. You both have answering services and so do I. You'll find a way to keep in touch." He glanced again at Valano. "You'll have to relieve Jake whenever he thinks you should. If we have any trouble tomorrow I'll get another man on it."

The telephone buzzed as he finished and when he answered Alice Maxwell said: "Mr. Clayton's on the wire," and Fenner said: "Put him on."

"Mr. Fenner?" Clayton said.

"Jack," said Fenner.

"All right, Jack. Mark Haskell will be out for most of the afternoon but they know he'll be back before the office closes at five because he's got some letters that'll be on his desk and need his signature."

"Okay. I have two men in my office now who'll take over so don't worry about it. One is an ex-cop named Jake Kinlaw," he said and went on to describe him; he did the same thing with Tom Valano. "But before you ring off there are a couple of things I should have asked you this morning. They could be a help. For instance what about Haskell's after-work habits, where does he usually eat, what does he do?"

"More often than not at the University Club." Clayton mentioned two other restaurants. "Sometimes ocke Ober's. Sometimes he'll have a girl with him but mostly he's playing bridge or billiards at the club until he goes home. As I told you, he's always been a cheater but there was one regular. I think, I'm pretty sure, her name is Sandra Joslin. I don't know where she lives but Marion Haskell could probably tell you because the investigator she hired to get divorce evidence turned her up. I don't know if it's still on, but up to two or three weeks ago this Joslin woman would either visit Mark or he'd bring her home with him. Once a week, always the same night. Tuesdays I think." He paused, then added, "And that's tonight, isn't it?"

The added information pleased Fenner and he said so. Then Clayton said: "How did Nancy Moore take to the girl you hired as a companion? Did they hit it off at lunch?"

Fenner said very well indeed, hung up, and turned back to Kinlaw and Valano. He relayed the information and Kinlaw nodded, his broad florid face bunching to narrow the small brown eyes.

"Should be a cinch," he said, the tone mildly lascivious. "If he's right about Tuesdays and Haskell's still working on the dame we should get a look at her. The only thing"—he turned to Valano—"is you may be out late."

Valano's grin was unperturbed. "That depends on what Haskell has in mind. If he wants a long session tonight he may bring her home early."

Kinlaw made a throaty noise that was difficult to diagnose and Fenner broke it up. He said they could take it from here and if they needed help to get in touch.

Kinlaw stood up, doubtful now. "Should I carry a piece?"

"That's up to you," Fenner said dryly. "You should know enough not to use it unless you're damn sure you won't have to face a grand jury."

"But what if we see," Valano said, "I mean, either of us, see Haskell approach Clayton some place?"

"Well, you'll be there, won't you? You won't need a gun to close in. Look, Haskell's not enough of a psycho to start shooting in front of witnesses. If it was that way all he'd have to do is step into Clayton's office anytime and put two or three slugs in him."

Valano nodded, still doubtful, but Kinlaw's, "sure," was confident and assured. Turning, he took Valano's arm and said: "Let's get with it, kid."

Fenner watched them close the door behind them and then sat down, ignoring for the moment the two telephone calls that had to be returned, while he reviewed the situation and wondered if it was time to call on Marion Haskell.

6

Jack Fenner made the telephone calls, one to an insurance investigator and one to a small law firm to report on the location of a witness they had been looking for. About to leave, he had a new thought that on further reflection seemed like a promising one. He asked Alice to call the *Courier* and see if Kent Murdock was in. Presently, when the familiar voice came to him, he said:

"Hi. How you doing these days?"

"About as usual I guess. You?"

"The same."

"Something on your mind?"

"In a way. I'd like some information and I don't want to intrude in that chicken coop you call an office."

Murdock gave a small audible snort and his tone became at once falsely formal.

"We have," he said, "a well-equipped and extensive library —still called by some the morgue—on the fourth floor, and an efficient and cooperative librarian. Certain privileged people are allowed to consult him. I might possibly arrange—"

Fenner cut him off. "What I want I doubt I'll find even in your superbly maintained stacks. What I need you'll have to get from your entertainment editor, or that guy that does the gossip column and covers the nightclub beat."

"You want gossip, not facts."

"Both if possible but I'll settle for some good rumors."

"Is there some small honorarium involved?"

"The honorarium is for you. Dinner tonight at Terroni's, including a brandy—on me."

"Correction. On some unsuspecting client."

Fenner laughed. "How well you know me, pal. But talk to some people, hunh? Snoop a bit. Like all you guys do."

"And pay off part-time snoopers to help them snoop. Who do I ask about?"

"A girl named Sandra Joslin. Address unknown at the moment. Probably a looker, possibly being kept by some local character. Known to visit Mark Haskell once a week at his apartment. Do you know him?"

"I know him—as well as I want to . . . Okay, I'll ask around. About dinner. Fine if it's not too late."

"How about seven sharp?"

"Seven will be fine."

The Stanton, located in the Kenmore district, was an apartment hotel whose guests were more residential and long-term than transient. The lobby was small, so was the reception desk. There was no doorman and the glass outer doors stood open, and Fenner came in briskly, nodded to the lone bored clerk, and moved unchallenged to the elevator.

The woman who opened the door to the third-floor apartment with some caution was about five-feet-six and weighed perhaps a hundred and twenty-five pounds. Casually dressed in well-cut blue slacks and an off-white turtleneck that did nice things for her figure, she had dark-brown hair that he guessed might show an auburn tinge in the proper light. Not pretty but with some basic inbred attractiveness, the hazel eyes inspected him doubtfully through the one-foot opening. Recognizing her but aware that she could not know him, he said, "Mrs. Haskell?"

Then he introduced himself and showed his identification. Still with some wariness and hesitation she finally spoke.

"How did you know where to find me?"

"Ben Clayton told me. I'm working for him as of this morning. He said it would be all right to stop by. I thought he might have phoned you."

"No." She shook her head, the bottom edges of her attractive hairdo swinging slightly. But she did open the door and step back and Fenner said, "Thank you," and moved past her into a small entryway. He stood waiting until she led the way into a comfortably furnished living room, well lighted but having no view of the river, and with a definite masculine tone.

When she had settled on the edge of the divan and he had taken a chair diagonally across from her she said: "Ben told you about Mark's threats? He hired you to—well, sort of protect him?"

"Something like that. Actually what we're doing at the moment is keeping an eye on Haskell. Mr. Clayton and his attorney told me about the board meeting Monday and the pressure put on you by your husband to get your proxy. He also said something about your being held a prisoner in your own house."

"Yes, that's true. He brought in some oversized masculine-looking woman to keep me locked in a room. Not mine, but one on the attic floor."

"If that's true how did you get out?"

For the first time she smiled and it had much to recommend it.

"When the woman came I suppose I guessed what Mark might have had in mind so right off we arranged—Ben and I—to have him phone me each morning at nine and each evening at the same hour. If I didn't answer or was unable to talk to him he'd know why. That's what happened."

The smile was small now but fixed, and her thoughts seemed a long way off, her tone quiet but with some tinge of admiration.

"You might not think so, but Ben can be quite determined

when he makes up his mind to. So he drove to Dedham rather early the morning after he was told I couldn't come to the phone. He parked down the street and watched the house until my guardian drove out to do her marketing; then he simply walked to the back door, broke a section of glass, and reached in to turn the key. He came right up, unlocked my door, and I packed a bag and well"—the eyes came back to him, still proud—"brought me here."

Fenner nodded, approval in his glance and liking her better all the time.

"Clayton told me you divorced him because you caught him with another woman."

She made a gesture of silent assent and sighed, her breasts beneath the turtleneck sagging slightly.

"I've done a lot of stupid silly things. But nothing to compare with that."

"He was in bed with some woman?"

"Not really. He was drunk and so was the girl, a little anyway. He was in his shorts and she was sitting across this table that had a lot of cards on it, also in her panties and bare above that, when Mark unlocked the door—it was the same apartment he still has —and we went in.

"I'd been spending the week on the Cape and he'd been after me, Mark, that is, for a long time insinuating this and that and daring me to come with him that night." She sighed again, a despairing sound, her eyes downcast and distance in her voice.

"I suppose I went there to prove, once and for all, that Ben would never do such a thing. I wouldn't listen when he told me it was the first time a thing like that had happened. I was so damn hurt and crushed and incredulous when I found him with that girl that I was ready to believe all the lies Mark fed me about Ben's other secret affairs. I couldn't think straight or rationalize. I suppose my false pride made me want to hit back, to get even . . . Oh, I don't know," she finished miserably, eyes bright with unwanted tears. "Why did you have to remind me?"

Her distress was genuine and Fenner was embarrassed and truly sorry. He said so.

"Believe me, I didn't mean to upset you, Mrs. Haskell. I was just trying to get—"

She waved him to silence and blinked the wetness from her eyes. "It's not your fault."

"Clayton says you married Haskell on the rebound."

"I guess you could call it that. He was always there. I don't know, maybe it was spite, some way of hurting Ben. And I knew within a month I'd made a ghastly mistake and I guess it was nothing but my stupid pride that made me stay with him all this time. Later when Mark saw how I felt about him he told me about how he'd arranged the trick he'd played on Ben. He even boasted about it.

"Mark had rented that apartment for some time, listing it as a company expense for entertainment purposes—until his father found out about it just before his death and made Mark pay the rent himself. And there was this man—I think his name was Bascomb—who worked as an advertising and public-relations man for the company. It seems part of his duties was to act as a procurer to provide attractive girls for out-of-town buyers.

"So this one time there was this buyer in town and the three men, Ben and Bascomb and this man, took three girls to dinner. They had a lot to drink. I don't know whether Ben was lonely or whether Bascomb made him think it was his duty to please the customer. Later the customer and his girl took off by themselves and Ben and Bascomb went to the apartment with their girls and Bascomb kept spiking Ben's drinks and got him into this strip-poker game. By the time we got there Bascomb and his girl were in one of the bedrooms and Ben was sitting there in his shorts with this pitiful silly grin on his face.

"You see," she said, "Mark made Bascomb arrange the whole thing, ordered him to if he wanted to keep his job. And then a few months later fired the poor man. It was characteristic of the way Mark is and I wasn't smart enough to know it."

"You were going to divorce Haskell?" Fenner said, starting to zero in on what he wanted most.

"Yes."

"You hired a private investigator. Do you recall his name?"

"A Mr. Glover. Fred Glover, I think."

"I know him. Was there a girl named Sandra Joslin involved?"

"Among others. Though I think she was the only regular."

"Do you know where she lives?"

"I'm sorry. I can't remember."

"But there was an address."

"I think so, yes."

"Did Glover give you a copy of his report?"

"Yes."

"Where is it?"

"In my room in Dedham, not the third-floor one, my bedroom. In the bottom drawer of a chest under some sweaters."

"Do you have a key to the house."

"Yes." She rose and left the room. When she returned she had a small key case. There were four keys and she indicated the proper one.

"Do I have your permission to get that report?"

"Certainly if you want it."

"Good." Fenner's smile was encouraging. "Now I'll need a to-whom-it-may-concern note authorizing me to enter the house and take the report . . . In case," he added, "your Amazon gives me an argument and threatens to call the law."

As was the custom when such houses were built, the Haskell residence stood rather close to the road, with a wide but shallow front yard, mostly planting and no more than six feet deep. The acreage, hedged-in at the sides, was at the rear and beyond was a patch of woods just as Nancy Moore had described it.

The basic architecture was what Fenner thought of as American Farmhouse, the clapboard construction, white-painted and green-trimmed now, a basic two-and-a-half-story box originally.

Two well-proportioned wings, slightly smaller, had been added later, the one on the right being a four-stall garage with living quarters above, apparently for the help when such help was available.

Having considered the open drive, Fenner decided to make his attack frontal. A wooden gate opened to his push and he went up four wide wooden steps to a handsome door topped with a lovely fanlight.

There was a bell and he pushed it as he reached for the key case. Not waiting, he unlocked the door and entered a broad entrance hall with a graceful curving staircase straight ahead. The Amazon appeared from some side room as he turned from closing the door.

The description, he decided, was apt. As tall as he was, she carried probably one hundred and sixty pounds on her muscular frame. The stern, unsmiling face was tight-lipped and pugnacious in that first moment of confrontation, the narrowed gaze outraged.

"How did you get in?" she demanded in her mannish baritone.

"With a key," Fenner said flatly, and displayed it. "Also an authorization from Mrs. Haskell to get something from her bedroom. Do you want to read it?"

"I most certainly do."

He let her read the note but snatched it back when she had finished. "Which is Mrs. Haskell's bedroom?"

"Find it yourself."

"Sure. Just come along with me, hunh? So I won't steal the family jewels."

He turned and started up the stairs which curved right partway up. The floors here, as they were on the first floor, were random width, waxed, and with a broad runner down the center. Marion Haskell's room was the second one he tried, and the report, on several typewritten pages, was right where she said it would be. Satisfied and ignoring the angry disapproval of the Amazon, he glanced about for a phone, located a jack but no instrument, which made him wonder if it had been purposely removed.

Starting back with the woman marching behind him, he reached the main hall, eyes still busy until he spotted the telephone and stand in a narrower hall leading to the rear and behind the staircase.

"I'm going to make a call," he told the woman. "You can listen if you like."

His indispensable notebook gave him the number he wanted but the voice that answered told him he had the answering service. Which did not surprise him. For Glover was an independent, part-time operator, a veteran of thirty years, most of them as a detective with the city police, who kept busy now not so much for fat fees as to fight off idleness. His work these days was mostly for legal firms, and that he had undertaken the Haskell assignment spoke of a solid recommendation from some firm of importance.

When Fenner had given his name he asked when Glover was expected.

"Probably late in the afternoon," the voice said. "Is there a message?"

"Yes. Tell him please that Jack Fenner called, and that if I don't get him later this afternoon I'll try him at home."

He hung up and faced the Amazon who stood almost at his elbow, her face frozen with disapproval and her glare fixed. As he stopped with his hand on the doorknob he was unable to resist a grin that was both deliberate and faintly mocking.

"Thank you, madam," he said, and gave her a small bow, "for your helpful cooperation."

7

Back in town Jack Fenner had one more thing he wanted to do before he tried Fred Glover again. From where he left his car in the parking lot near his office it was but a four-block walk to the Edwards Building, a creaking ten-story structure that had somehow survived its more modern surroundings. The two elevators were cages presided over by uniformed ancients and it took a long time for a complete round trip.

The directory board in the lower hall told him he wanted six fourteen and when he reached it he saw six names lettered on the frosted-glass upper half of the door. Since no professions were mentioned it was assumed that callers knew whom they wanted to see and the nature of the business to be conducted.

The door opened directly into one good-sized room with a small alcove just inside where a galvanized, unpainted steel bar supported several coat hangers, none of them in use, with a shelf above. There were, he saw, six desks in two rows, the lucky three having the two windows on their side. Three were empty. At one of the others the owner was just putting on his jacket, apparently through for the day. As he advanced he could see the nameplates that identified each occupant and he took a chance and moved toward the window desks. At the rearmost one a man slouched in his chair, feet on the windowsill and felt hat tipped over his eyes; at the middle one a gaunt-looking fellow with thinning mousy hair and hollow cheeks was working at a typewriter.

Fenner approached this one with fingers crossed, and again his luck was in for the nameplate read: HARRY F. BASCOMB. The typewriter continued to chatter as he stopped by the lone straight-backed chair at the end of the desk. He had already noticed that each desk was similarly supplied, and he had time to wonder what the arrangement was if more than one client appeared at the same time before the typing stopped and Harry Bascomb glanced up.

The eyes that made that first quick inspection were amber-colored and busy in their appraisal. The dark-rimmed glasses with the wide sidebows magnified the look slightly. There was a worn, gray tweed jacket draped over the customer's chair, the slacks were mostly hidden, but the shirt, open at the throat, was wide-striped and somewhat frayed at the cuffs.

The smile came quickly then, genuine enough but not without some hint of suspicion. Fenner returned it and said: "Harry Bascomb?"

"Right. Hi."

Bascomb jumped up then and Fenner saw the slacks were gray flannel and well wrinkled. The jacket was whisked from the chair back and the seat made available.

"Sit down, sit down. Mr.—ah—"

"Fenner. Jack Fenner. You do publicity, that sort of thing?"

"I do indeed." The corner of the mouth twisted. "Though we prefer a somewhat more professional term."

"Like public relations?"

"Exactly. Are you in need of such? What is *your* line Mr. Fenner?"

"I'm a private investigator."

The announcement apparently came as something of a shock because the hope that was flowering faded almost immediately leaving the gaze flat and disinterested. At that Bascomb made some polite show of interest.

"Did you have some bit of advertising in mind? Perhaps some little scheme whereby we could publicize your name or business?"

"What I have in mind," Fenner said, pleasantly but succinctly, "is some information, Harry."

Bascomb glanced out the window, held the pose a few seconds, brought the eyes back to the half-finished sheet in the typewriter. When he was ready he looked right at Fenner and said:

"As you can see I'm rather busy, Mr. Fenner. A rush job for a regular client."

"What you mean is that you expect to be paid for your time."

"If you put it that way"—there must have been some irrepressible quality in Harry Bascomb because the lip-quirk came back—"yes."

"Fine. I get paid for my time, why shouldn't you?"

"Well, that is different," Bascomb said, his tone warming again. "I must say I like your attitude. That is"—and so fleeting was the hope that it again started to fade—"if I have the information you happen to want."

"If I didn't think you had I wouldn't be here. But just to be sure, did you once work for Haskell & Company?"

This time the mouth dipped in quick resentment. "At one time, yes."

"Then you're my man." Fenner pulled his chair a few inches closer. "My sources gave me a story today and all I want from you is some confirmation. Any additional angles could mean a few extra bucks. It goes like this, Harry."

Fenner told the story well and by the visible response—the occasional nod, the deepening of the resentment—he was sure it was the right one. When he finished Bascomb swore softly but with great conviction.

"I don't know where you got the information but it's the McCoy. That sonofabitch," he added viciously but with some ambiguity. "That miserable bastard."

"Who?"

"Mark Haskell. Christ, you ought to know who."

"Okay, okay," Fenner said soothingly, concealing his amusement at Bascomb's gift for profanity. "I was told you set Ben Clayton up, also that you made a damn fine job of it."

"All right, I did . . . Let me ask you something Fenner"—he had forgotten the mister—"did you ever do something you regretted, I don't mean constantly, every time you thought of it?"

"Luckily not very often, but I know what you mean."

"Well what I did that night was one of those things."

"What did Haskell tell you that made you the key man in that frame? Or did he just order you to?"

"Both. He was a convincing bastard when he put his mind to it. Said I'd have a fat raise the first of the year . . ."

"Convincing how, Harry?"

"Said Mrs. Clayton had been unhappy a long time and was desperate to get some useful divorce evidence; said Clayton had been cheating secretly for years . . . Well, how was I to know?"

"And it was the boss talking."

"Right."

"You were the company advertising manager?"

"And handled public relations. Mostly that. Advertising budget wasn't much because we didn't make a consumer product; what we did spend on advertising was in trade journals, industrial magazines. Mostly I knocked out squibs for the financial columnists, prepared quarterly reports, like that. Also I was," he added with some bitterness, "in charge of entertainment and procuring for the out-of-town clientele —and Haskell himself.

"This apartment thing was his idea, charged it to the company for entertainment purposes and kept it from the old man. So it was no problem to fix up Ben with a date when this other customer came to town. A family man from St. Louis who liked chicks. I lined up three, a hundred bucks apiece, and we went out to dinner. Haskell had already laid it out for me so later I tipped off the waiter, told him when we ordered drinks that Ben was to get doubles while the rest of us got the usual."

He paused, mouth tightening at the corners, the amber eyes remote and unhappy.

"By the time we'd finished nightclubbing Ben had a load. The customer split and the four of us went to the apartment. I suppose you know about the strip-poker game? . . . Well, I was in one of the bedrooms with my girl when the plug was pulled, but I found out later that Ben was down to his shorts and the girl in nothing but panties when Haskell brought the wife in."

Fenner waited awhile, seeing the depression set in; then he said: "Did you get the raise?"

The question snapped Bascomb out of it. "Raise hell! A couple, three months later I got the boot, that's what I got. By that time Ben was already divorced and Haskell was hanging around Marion. Haskell told me to get lost. Ben never tumbled to the frame until he was divorced. Haskell told him just so he could rub it in. Which is just what a mean unscrupulous bastard like him would do. So there's no way I could ever get a good reference from either Haskell or Clayton.

"Since then it's been rough, believe me. Scratch along, a client here a client there. Mostly for nickels and dimes. A couple restaurants, a nightclub that needs some publicity puffs, some no-talent entertainers, now and then a second-rate fighter . . ." He seemed to run out of words and spirit then and Fenner stood up.

He took a silver money clip from his pocket. He had had it designed so that a dog tag helped make up one side, a reminder of Korea and of no other practical use except that his blood type was stamped in the metal. He slipped out the folded bills, removed a new twenty, and put it on the desk.

"I used up about a half hour," he said. "At that rate you make more than I do. Now you can buy some prospective client a dinner."

Bascomb looked at the bill but did not touch it. When his eyes came up they were pleased and, somehow, grateful. But he'd been kicked around too long to come out with a straightforward thanks; so he shrugged and said:

"Maybe so, Mr. Fenner, maybe so. I only wish I had your expense account . . . Appreciate it. You need anything in my line, stop by, hunh?"

8

Jack Fenner reached Fred Glover at his home just before he left to keep his dinner date with Kent Murdock. With the amenities over, he said he was doing some work for Esterbrook & Warren and had in his hand a copy of the report made for Marion Haskell, adding that he had it with her permission.

"Well, if you read it, Jack," Glover said with some amusement, "you know what the score is, don't you?"

"Basically, yes. But knowing how thorough you are I have an idea you could tell me a few things that weren't in that report because they weren't particularly pertinent."

"What do you have in mind?"

"I'm interested in this Joslin woman who was visiting Haskell's apartment one night a week. Always on Tuesday, right?"

"If that's what my report says."

"You wanted evidence Mrs. Haskell could use, but I know damn well you asked some questions of the help, if only to get a better idea of the setup the Joslin girl had."

"Like for instance?"

"Did she have many callers?"

"No."

"Did Haskell ever go there?"

"No."

"But someone did. Always the same guy?"

"Always."

"How often?"

"Maybe a couple of times a week for a before-dinner drink, but only once a week to get what he was probably paying for. Occasionally he'd take her to dinner, come back with her, be out of there by one or two in the morning. More often they ate at her place but he'd still leave about the same time."

"So she has her guy at her place one night a week, but goes to Haskell's on Tuesdays."

"She did during the time I was on the case."

"Why? How could she be sure that her boyfriend would not stop in unexpectedly on Tuesdays?"

"Because that's the night for this high-stake poker game that has been floating around town for years."

"I've heard about it," Fenner said. "Now for the jackpot question. Who's the guy?"

"Monty Saxton."

"Oh-ho . . . And he was paying the rent?"

"The rent was paid the first of the month in cash."

"Would it be fair to assume it was taken care of by her regular visitor?"

"You *could* assume that. But I wouldn't go around assuming it in public. Monty's a married man with a couple of kids in college."

"Yeah." Fenner considered what he knew about the man and his background and was ready to agree. "You could be right. Did you get around to finding out if she had a bank account?"

"She did. Maybe four months old. Four figures is all the bank would say. So you can take your choice of any number from a thousand to, say, ninety-five hundred."

"And she dressed well."

"I thought so. Had a very nice-looking mink coat back in February when I was interested in her."

"Thanks, Fred. I owe you one."

"I'll make a note of it."

.   .   .

Terroni's had long had a reputation as one of the better eating places in town and nothing had changed that Fenner could see since his first meal there. There were no frills like padded and upholstered bar stools, or banquettes, or subdued lighting. It was all out in the open, the lighting good so the fish-eaters would not get a bone by mistake. The tables were white-topped and bare except for condiments; some time after you sat down a paper place mat and silver would be furnished but the napkins were linen and crisply laundered.

Fenner was near the front end of the bar on the left, one foot on the rail, weight on the other foot, and hunched slightly with shoulders turned fractionally to watch the entrance. He had taken the first small savoring sip of his dry martini with a twist when he spotted Kent Murdock swing in off the sidewalk. And now he caught the bartender's eye.

"Send another one of these over to the table, Frank." He indicated the wall table he had spoken for. "Have the girl put it on the dinner check."

When he was sure Murdock had seen him he started diagonally across the room, pointing with the glass. Murdock got the message and they met at the table. Here Fenner put down his glass, and because they had not seen each other in perhaps three weeks, they shook hands.

Standing together like that, and not counting faces—Fenner's was a bit more angular—they looked strikingly similar physically. Perhaps a fraction of an inch difference in height and five pounds in weight, with Fenner seeming slightly leaner; the same good shoulders and no noticeable bulge at the waist. Murdock's hair was thicker, with a slight wave, and noticeably graying while Fenner's was still black, parted in the middle, and with widow's peaks that gave him an appearance vaguely similar to some artists' conception of Mephistopheles. The eyes too were different, Fenner's green ones alert and observing and often tinged with suspicion while Murdock's dark gaze, equally shrewd, was somewhat more tolerant.

When the waitress came with Murdock's drink, she also brought the paper place mats and silver, slapping the well-worn menus in front of them. Middle-aged and husky, with tinted hair, she had developed an outspoken manner that, over the years, had come to verge on the insolent. Now she said;

"You want to order now or have another drink?"

"Bring another one of these in ten minutes, Grace," Fenner said, "and then we'll give you an order."

They talked about this and that, catching up on things, until the second drink came and Grace demanded an order.

"Lobster, broiled," Murdock said without consulting the menu. "A pound and a quarter to a half."

"Lobster?" Fenner said in mock outrage.

"What's the matter?"

"The matter is that they are scarce as hell right now and the prices are out of sight. Look at the menu. They're afraid to state a price. Just that 'according to size' bit. Right, Grace?"

Grace answered with a disdainful shrug and Murdock, grinning now, said: "Who's paying for this?"

Fenner stared a moment, then winked. "Is the swordfish fresh, Grace?"

"Fresh?" said Grace. "Are you crazy? You know swordfish don't come this far north, or even Montauk, until summer. They were fresh when we froze them. Sure. What do you think?"

"Just bring a slab, also broiled," Fenner said. "With a baked potato, mixed green—no make that lettuce and tomatoes—with oil and vinegar, and coffee later, okay?"

"Two," Murdock said.

"You want something first?" Grace picked up the menus. "Maybe a cup of chowder, Mr. Murdock, because you know, we don't precook our lobsters and slap them under a broiler to reheat them; we start with them live. It'll take maybe twenty, twenty-five minutes."

"I'll nurse this." Murdock tapped his martini glass and when Grace left he added: "You sure have a nice touch with waitresses."

"It's my winning personality. Have you got any goodies for me?"

"It depends on what you already have."

"Gimmee."

Murdock waited until he had a cigarette going. "Your Sandra has been seen around but not too often. A big blond and built —I think I've seen her myself—and almost always alone. A couple of times having an early dinner with Monty Saxton. One of our guys spotted her once with Mark Haskell at some out-of-the-way restaurant. No nightclub regular. Seen a couple of times at Suffolk Downs and once at Narragansett. The only regular appearance is the home hockey games. Same seat, a good one, and since there are no good ones available except to season ticket holders, someone gives it to her."

He paused to see how his information was being accepted and saw that Fenner's gaze was steady and bright with interest.

"They say Saxton brought her up from New Orleans some months ago and there's a good reason why he keeps her pretty well hidden and is seldom seen with her. He's under a federal indictment for income-tax evasion and a lot of his investments and holdings were placed in his wife's name some time ago. She could really put him in a bind if she clamped down on him or sued for divorce . . . Have you ever seen them out together?"

Fenner nodded, knowing what Murdock meant. Mrs. Saxton, he thought her name was Sylvia, was a plump petite brunette with nice ankles and tiny feet. She seemed always to be in charge when Fenner had seen the two out together, and it was quite obvious that in such cases Saxton was dutifully attentive for a middle-aged married man and made sure that her whims and wishes were taken care of.

"Saxton has to go to out-of-town meetings from time to time," Murdock continued, "and the rumor is that the wife doesn't care if he beds down now and then with some call girl so long as he doesn't make a regular thing out of it. Apparently she nearly kicked him out some time back when he'd set up a girl on a semipermanent basis."

The food came to punctuate the statement and for a while then they were busy doing justice to it. What talk there was took the form of brief comments and half sentences and contented grunts. When Grace came to clear off she asked if they wanted their coffee now.

"Please," said Fenner. "And two Remy Martins."

"A pony or a drink?"

"A drink," Murdock said. "And Mr. Fenner will take the check."

Relaxed with their brandies, Murdock broke the silence. He'd been watching his friend, eyes half closed and head slightly tipped.

"Is it all right to ask who you're working for?"

"Indirectly for Esterbrook & Warren."

"Hmm. A high-class job. And why the interest in Mark Haskell?"

Fenner told him about the board meeting and Haskell's efforts to block the takeover. "When Haskell found out he might be out of a job he flipped. He's also been threatening his one-time buddy Ben Clayton because Clayton is the one who started the negotiations."

"Threatened? Threatened to what?"

"Kill him."

Murdock scowled skeptically and abandoned his somewhat artificial accent.

"Oh, come off it, Jack. And Clayton takes it seriously?"

"Maybe he should."

"But—I thought, like you said, they were long-time buddies."

"They were when they were young. Clayton's term was 'toady and paid companion' and he hates himself now for sucking along for so many years. You'd have to know the background to understand. Also, Haskell has been harassing his half sister—name of Nancy Moore from the Coast—who'd been missing for twenty years and was located on old man Haskell's instructions about a month ago."

"Why? What sort of harassment?"

Fenner told him and added: "If the takeover goes through Haskell gets between three and four million but he's out of his hundred-and-twenty-five-grand-a-year job. The Moore girl came into twenty-four percent of the stock under the old man's will. With her vote or proxy Haskell can probably block the takeover . . . She won't play."

"So Clayton really thinks Haskell might knock him off? And you're giving him some protection, is that it?"

"In a way."

"Isn't there a Mrs. Haskell?"

"There is."

"A nice-looking girl, gives the impression she has a lot of class."

"Agreed."

"And wasn't she once married to Ben Clayton?"

"She was."

"Ahh. And could this personal element enter into the problem?"

"It could and does." Fenner took his last sip of brandy, glanced at the check and reached for his wallet. "It seems," he added, "that Clayton spirited—to coin a word—Mrs. Haskell away from the Dedham home where Haskell was keeping her on ice and he doesn't know where Clayton took her. She also owns some stock."

"Am I permitted to ask a couple more questions?"

"You are."

"Do you think Haskell has been fooling with Saxton's girl?"

"It's a possibility."

"He has to know who he might have to tangle with."

"Probably. The trouble is that I've heard that Haskell has been a semiregular in those floating Tuesday night, high-stake poker games."

"I heard that," Murdock said. "Also that he's a lousy player and has a few large IOUs floating around and that Saxton has been putting some pressure on him."

"Thanks. That I didn't know." Fenner watched Grace put

down his change and waved it away. He was silent another minute, chasing thoughts around inside his head and seeing possible complications he hadn't counted on . . . "What?" he said.

"I said"—Murdock's dark eyes were amused—"I have a hunch that says you are going to pay the Joslin girl a visit."

"A distinct possibility. Why?"

Murdock glanced at his watch and said, offhandedly and still amused: "Oh, I just thought if you were going now I could make a phone call, postpone my date a half hour or so, and tag along."

Fenner grunted. "I don't think so."

"That I can't go, or that you're not going to see her?"

"I have an idea I'd better do some thinking first. Also the morning might be better. I don't know that I'd like to be chatting away tonight with Miss Joslin and have Monty Saxton drop in unexpectedly, you know?"

Murdock said he knew and pushed his chair back. He asked Fenner if his investment in the dinner was worthwhile and Fenner said adequately.

9

Jack Fenner had just finished making his second and last drink —the doctor had said a drink or two before turning in was better for him than a sleeping capsule—and was about to enjoy the last side of a stack of records he had put on when there was a loud and intent knocking on his door.

He wasn't sure of the time, and didn't bother to look, but thought it might be eleven or a bit earlier. He had come home around nine, removed his jacket, loosened his collar and tie and put on slippers. He had thought about building a fire but decided it was too much effort for such a short time, so he had read the papers, put the records on, and let his mind drift, aware again how much he liked the room and noting with some pleasure the prints on the walls—a John Sloan, two Reginald Marshes, a Gordon Grant, and a copy of a famous George Bellows depicting two club fighters slugging it out in the ring. The record, an oldie and one of his favorites, featured George Van Eps on his special guitar and backed with tasteful arrangements by a big-band accompaniment.

Before that he had played and thoroughly enjoyed some Art Tatum. For him there was only one word for the man—unbelievable—and because nobody before or since could play that left hand he often wished he could have lived forever. There were, and had been, others that did okay: Fats Waller, Teddy Wilson, Herman Chittison, Dick Hyman, and for barrelhouse, Ralph Sutton. Oscar Peterson maybe, though if he had any confidence and thought he could cut it alone why did he depend on his sidemen—bass and drums—when Tatum needed nobody?

Now, irritated at the interruption, he listened to eight more bars of Van Eps on *Sweet Lorraine* before he rose and walked to the door. The pounding had started again and he opened the door with a jerk; then stopped, mouth half open, and stared at a Ben Clayton he had never seen before. It was not just the whisky breath that nearly knocked him over, or the crimson face; it was the state of dishevelment so out of character as to be, momentarily at least, quite incredible.

Although Clayton still wore the shirt and tie, which was badly askew, his business suit and vest had given way to slacks and worn loafers and an old tweed coat, one side of which sagged noticeably. The prematurely gray hair was mussed and wispy, the mouth slack, the bleary light-brown eyes peering vacantly at him behind the metal-rimmed spectacles.

"Hi, Jack," he said thickly, and grinned foolishly. "You said to call you Jack, didn't you? Okay to come in? I have to talk to you, it's important."

Fenner sighed resignedly and stepped back while Clayton headed unsteadily for the davenport. There was a round-backed Windsor chair nearby and now he removed his jacket and slung it over the back. As he did so there was the distinct sound of some hard and heavy object in one of the pockets banging once against the side of the chair.

Hearing this and remembering the sag in the jacket when Clayton entered, Fenner seemed to understand in quick alarm that there was a gun in that pocket. He watched Clayton slump down on the davenport and said, knowing even then what he might have to do:

"Let me get you a drink, Ben. I was just having a nightcap. Scotch or Bourbon."

"Brandy, old boy. And not too weak, understand?"

When Fenner came back from the kitchen Clayton's eyes were half-closed, but he roused himself quickly when he reached for the glass, took a large swallow, and said: "Ahh—had to talk to you." He put the glass on the coffee table. "Had an idea tonight. Like to know what you think of it."

"How many drinks before you got this idea?"

"Oh, just a few." The tone was cagey. "You see, Mark is going to kill me sometime between now and Monday. Remember, we talked about that. The guy has flipped, and he's gonna make me pay because he knows he's gonna get the boot from his cushy job as soon as the board meeting is over."

"He'll still get three to four million in stock."

" 'S not the money. Pride. Got to have revenge, make me pay cause I started it all. One hundred and twenty-five thousand a year," he said resentfully, "and me getting forty-five and doing all the work. Well, so I got this idea, a sure way to keep him from killing me, and maybe even Marion if he finds her."

"How?"

"Simple." The wet lips grinned crookedly and the eyes were crafty. "Kill him first! How about that for an idea? If old Mark is dead he can't kill me, can he?"

For long moments Fenner just looked down at him. He took an uneasy breath and let it out slowly, knowing somehow that the man meant it, knowing too that the best way to stop him was to get him drunk and keep him here all night. So intent was he on the possible ramifications of the thought that he missed something Clayton had said and had to force his mind back to the present.

"Sorry, Ben. I was—"

"I said, don't you like the idea?"

Fenner made his voice deliberately flat and offensive. "To put it briefly, no."

"Why?"

"Because you'll wind up doing twenty years in prison the hard way."

"Not if I get away with it." Clayton tried to sit erect and gave up. "Look," he continued with some alarm as a new and apparently disturbing thought came to him, "you don't have to tell the police what I've said, do you?"

"Not until they find Haskell murdered and start asking around."

"But I thought—I thought—whatever I told you was in confidence. That's why I decided to come here."

"Confidence, yes."

"Well, then—"

"But any communication we have is not *legally* privileged."

"Not like between a lawyer and his client?"

"No."

"Oh."

Fenner paused, trying to guess how drunk the man was. "I can't be made to tell the police or even the district attorney what you tell me, but a judge would have me in a cell unless I came clean. Also if you kill Haskell and get caught—"

"I'm not planning to get caught," Clayton said stubbornly, the words still slurring.

"—and are convicted—do you hear me?"

"I hear you, I hear you. If I get caught and convicted—"

"Then my withholding evidence and obstructing the investigation could make me an accessory before and possibly after the fact."

"Let's have a drink." Clayton roused himself again and held out his nearly empty glass. "Got to think this thing out."

Fenner's only comment was a mental one which said, Gladly, pal, gladly . . .

Coming back to the davenport with a purposely strong drink, Fenner thought his guest might be asleep, but Clayton, whose chin nearly touched his chest, snapped it up. He grinned wetly, took a swallow, and bobbed his head uncertainly in approval.

"That's a drink," he said, putting the glass down. "The kind I like. So let's go over this brilliant idea once more, okay?"

"Sure. When do you plan to do the job?"

"Well, I thought maybe tonight if I get my courage up, but anyway sometime soon. Can't give old Mark a chance to get me first, can I? That'd be kind of stupid . . ."

He said other things, some difficult to understand. Fenner listened, nodding encouragement as the voice droned on to become more and more confused and indistinct. Fenner saw the change happen before his eyes, though it took a few seconds to accept and understand it.

For suddenly the stubbornness was gone, the defiance with it. The facial muscles seemed to crumble one by one as they dissolved in slackness; at the same time tears began to well up in the dulled light-brown eyes.

"Maybe I don't care if I don't get away with it," Clayton said in a thick and bitter voice. "He's had it coming. If not from me from someone else he hurt. I should have done it the night he brought Marion to the apartment. Maybe I would have if I hadn't been so drunk. The sonofabitch. Did I tell you what he did?" he asked plaintively, the voice now a husky tremolo as some memory came flooding back.

Fenner, about to say he'd heard the story from Marion Haskell, shut his mouth. Let him talk, the poor guy. The more talk the more thirsty and the more drinks, and the quicker his own relief. *Just let's not have a crying jag,* he thought.

"He set me up, the sonofabitch, deliberately. He and another bastard and flunky named Harry Bascomb." He seemed to run down for a moment in his sadness and Fenner prompted him.

"You said something about Haskell catching you bare-assed with some girl."

"Wasn't bare-assed." Clayton, aware of his tears was trying to blink them away. "Almost though, I guess," he added honestly. "In my shorts, the girl too. Bascomb and his girl were in the bedroom. Maybe I *would* have been bare-assed, maybe I'd've been in bed if they'd come a bit later. I was too drunk to do anything anyway but fumble around."

He removed his glasses and wiped both eyes with the back

of his right hand. With that he seemed to regain some control even though he still had trouble with his voice.

"Sorry about that," he said, his glance embarrassed. "Didn't mean to blubber, and anyway, that's not the point. If I'd ever cheated, or if Marion had been suspicious and hired someone like you or the man she got, then maybe I could say it served me right. But Mark was supposed to be a friend—"

He faltered and tried again. "No, I guess I knew he wasn't by then. But he didn't *happen* to come in with Marion; he *brought* her all the way from the Cape; he got Bascomb to get me drunk and provide the girls; then he walks in with a key . . ."

His voice trailed off at that point and he was now so slouched as to be almost on his back. Then, just when Fenner thought he was about to fold completely, he somehow jerked himself to a sitting position, pushed down with both hands, gave a loud and tortured groan, and managed to stagger upright. He blinked owlishly, replaced his glasses, steadied himself, and said:

"Got to go to the john. Which way?"

Fenner steered him toward the bedroom, grateful for the respite. He saw him safely inside and then wheeled, three long strides bringing him to the Windsor chair and tweed jacket. An instant later he had slipped the gun from the side pocket. It was a .38 in good condition with a two-inch barrel, fully loaded.

Flipping out the cylinder, he tipped the shells into his palm and then went quickly through the other pockets. The inside pocket held a coat wallet and one of those thin, cheap pens made by the Frenchman who had come over to challenge for the America's Cup and failed to make it; the two side pockets yielded the silver Zippo, a paper folder of matches, a pack of cigarettes somewhat squashed and half empty.

He had the gun back in the pocket when Clayton came weaving into the room, turned, and dropped on the davenport so heavily he bounced. He took another sip of his drink and peered at Fenner.

"Fix that drink of yours. Can't expect your guest to drink alone."

Fenner laughed at him. "And you don't expect me to catch up with you, do you?"

"Just fix that drink, hunh? And don't think you can cheat because I'm gonna taste it when you come back . . . Understand?" he added cunningly.

Fenner sighed and stood up. What a man had to do these days to earn a buck. He would, he guessed, have something of a hangover in the morning but he could think of other times and other hangovers that were worse than this one would be. He made the drink, his regular two-ounce portion, and came back to find Clayton lowering his glass and wiping his chin with the back of his hand. He had about an inch of drink left and he reached for Fenner's glass, grinning foolishly, eyes almost shut. To humor him Fenner let him taste his own drink and watched Clayton lean forward to fumble a cigarette from his jacket, spin flame from the Zippo, and then ruin the cigarette by holding the flame halfway to the end. He managed two puffs, saw what he had done, and dropped the remains disgustedly in the ashtray.

Even sitting up his torso was weaving, and finally he lifted his chin with an effort, put one finger alongside his nose and said slyly: "You know something, Jack? I think I'm a little drunk. Maybe I should let old Mark live another day."

"Why don't you stretch out for a few minutes and see how it goes."

"But just for a little while, hunh? You'll wake me, say in a couple of hours?"

"Sure."

"You got a blanket and a spare pillow?" He tugged at his tie, opened the collar, and kicked off his loafers. "Don't want to be any trouble, old buddy."

"Coming up," Fenner said, thankful that his plan had worked.

When Fenner returned Clayton was half lying down, his feet still on the floor. He sat up with an effort to let Fenner place the pillow and snap the blanket open. He reached for the remainder of his drink, started to toss it back, spotted Fenner's unfinished drink and stopped.

"C'm on," he said sternly. "Last drink. No heeltaps. Hate guys that waste good whisky."

Fenner sighed again, grinned, and thought, *What the hell? It won't kill me.*

He held his glass in a toasting position, said, "Cheers," and took five fast swallows, leaving the last inch in the glass. "That's it," he said. "Come on, get your feet up; it's getting late."

Clayton obeyed. He mumbled something about Fenner being a good guy, sighed heavily and turned on his side, his back to the room.

In the bedroom Fenner undressed, aware for the first time that the whisky was having some effect. He washed, and brushed his teeth, and then, barefoot and in shorts, he went back into the living room. He stood a moment over Clayton and said, softly: "Ben." Then louder: "Hey, Ben!"

When the other's breathing continued heavy and regular he took one shoulder and shook it gently. It was like shaking a soft two-hundred-pound hunk of flesh. Satisfied, he went about turning off lights. He started to close the bedroom door and then left it open, the thought occurring to him that if Clayton got sick during the night he might need some help . . .

When Jack Fenner first opened his eyes he sensed that it was some time before dawn, and when he rolled over, the bedside clock told him it was nearly five-thirty. There was a definite lethargy and logginess in his body that still demanded sleep but strangely his mind was quite alert. It was this awareness that started the chain of thoughts that led presently to the memory of what had happened in the living room some hours earlier. His reaction was immediate as he scrambled to his feet and just as suddenly he was scared.

Clayton and that damn gun! The shells in Fenner's coat pocket. *Suppose Clayton had been acting. Unlikely but possi-*

*ble. Suppose he had sneaked out to look for Mark Haskell with
an empty gun and —*

He stopped thinking, not wanting to go on. Instead he
stepped directly to the living room and moved naked and
barefoot toward the davenport. Because the gray of the ap-
proaching dawn had not yet reached the room he had to go
halfway across it before he could be sure that anyone was
there. When he saw the blanketed figure, the back and fanny
still turned toward him, relief came quickly and he felt an odd
weakness in his legs.

The breath he had been holding came out noisily and he
stood where he was for another minute until he was sure of his
guest's breathing that now had a distinct purring quality. Satisfied, the relief still with him, he turned back, his annoyance
starting to build because he had let his imagination run away
with his judgment.

Minutes after he had snuggled down in the still warm bed he
was asleep and when he again awoke the room was bright and
he felt rested and content. As he swung his feet over the side
he became aware of the slight hangover but decided he was
lucky it was no worse. No longer worried about Clayton he put
on his slippers and robe, belting it about him and figuring out
an acceptable schedule. In the living room once more he took
Clayton, who seemed not to have moved, by the shoulder and
shook him firmly. This time there was a grunting, groaning
response.

"Come on, Ben!" he said bluntly. "On your feet!"

Clayton hunched over on his back, the light-brown eyes without the necessary glasses staring owlishly until they focused.

"Oh." His normally placid face looked wan and sick but he
tried to cover up, speaking with forced cheerfulness. "Hi, Jack.
Wow! Have I got a head."

"Yeah." Fenner chuckled. "And you sure as hell earned it.
Come on, it's nine o'clock. Can you use an electric razor?"

"Sure."

"Go ahead."

"What about you?" Clayton sat up, stretched, yawned widely, and groped for his glasses. "I mean I don't want to—"

"I'll take my turn later. I want to shower too and there's no point in holding you up. I can offer only juice and coffee—instant."

"That's all I could get down anyway."

"Then go ahead. I'll put the water on."

He stood while Clayton put on his loafers and pushed off the davenport; then started purposefully toward the bedroom.

Fenner was not quite sure what prompted him to make his next move. He knew somehow that the crazy thought had been in the back of his mind ever since his relief had overcome him when he saw Clayton still on the davenport in the half-light of dawn. Perhaps it was the drilled-in habit acquired over the years never to accept the obvious; possibly some basic quirk of character, some inbred quality of suspicion was at fault. Whatever the reason, he stepped quickly to Clayton's jacket and lifted the revolver.

For just as the thought had injected itself that Clayton might have tricked him and gone hunting for Haskell with an empty gun, the counterthought came: *That Clayton had extra shells, had used the gun during the night, and returned unheard, counting on him, Fenner, for an alibi.*

He was ashamed of himself the moment he flipped out the cylinder and found it empty. Yet because he still could not let the insidious thought go, he glanced about, tore a jagged piece of white space from the nearest magazine. Then, reversing the gun, he held the white paper in front of the firing pin to reflect light and peered down the barrel. There was a patch of corrosion, apparently from previous neglect, but except for two tiny bits of lint that had clung there the inside was about as clean and shiny as it had ever been.

Sheepishly he flipped the cylinder in place, replaced the gun, and straightened, satisfied at last that it had not been used. His relief brightened the morning, his grin was unconscious, and he was not even aware that he was humming one of George Van

Eps' tunes of last night as he turned on the burner and ran water for the coffee . . .

Fenner had the coffee and juice on a tray when Clayton came back to the living room. He looked some better but not much. He still hadn't buttoned his collar but his gray hair was carefully combed and he smelled of after-shave lotion. Lifting his jacket from the chair he slipped it on, found a cigarette. He spun the Zippo wheel three times but all he got was sparks so he fumbled out the paper matches and finally got his light.

"What the hell was I drinking last night?" he asked ruefully.

"Brandy."

"Brandy? My God! I never drink it when I'm sober because I know it knocks me for a loop."

"You demanded it," Fenner said with some amusement.

"I would . . . Well—" He eased down on the edge of the davenport and reached for his glass of juice, downing it in two gulps. The hand that reached for the cup and saucer shook alarmingly and he had to steady it with his other hand before he could sip his coffee.

"Anyway," he said finally. "I'm glad I came, and thanks, Jack. Sorry to have been such a damn nuisance."

Fenner told him to forget it and asked if Clayton would be able to make it to the office. Clayton grinned and said he guessed he could hold out until Bloody Mary time.

10

Fenner stopped off at Mark Haskell's apartment on his way to his office. At that hour there were plenty of parking spaces and he spotted Tom Valano in his sporty hardtop and pulled in in front of him. As he approached, the young photographer, pantomiming, stuck a camera out of the lowered window and pretended to take a picture. Fenner asked what time he had come on and Valano said seven-thirty.

"What about last night? You picked Haskell up at his office?"

"Right. Followed him to the University Club." He grunted good-naturedly and digressed. "I'm glad Jake's taking over this tailing bit, it's not my bag."

Fenner nodded understandingly. "How long was he there?"

"Until about seven-thirty. Went from there to a little restaurant on Pratt Street. When he came out about nine or so he had a blond doll with him, a good-sized broad with a yummy figure. I figured she was there waiting for him, or else it was a pickup. Anyway he brought her home and Jake took over."

"Did he give you a rundown on the other tenants when he took over?"

Valano shook his head. "I forgot to ask him." He tapped a camera. "But so far I've got two women in their forties that could be schoolteachers. A couple, maybe around thirty, looked like business people. An airline stewardess, an old guy with a kind of shopping basket. He just came back again . . . And look, Jack," he added plaintively. "When's Kinlaw supposed to show? Wasn't he supposed to take over days and let me work nights?"

Fenner tapped Valano lightly on the shoulder. "Patience, son. Maybe he misunderstood me yesterday. I'll check when I get back to the office. How about if we make the change at noon, since you're already here. That way you'll be free for lunch and an early dinner before you have to take over again. I'll let you know." . . .

Alice Maxwell gave Fenner her customary bright smile and a cheerful good morning as she handed him a half dozen letters and two circulars. He didn't ask about coffee because she had never failed to provide it once they had set the original ground rules. Now, in his own office, he sat down, dismissing thoughts of Jake Kinlaw for the moment as he reached for a buttered Danish neatly done in waxed paper. When he had unwrapped it and tried a bite, he took the paper cup and pulled out the handles. The coffee, light and without sugar, was in a green thermos carafe on a side table, and after two satisfying swallows he examined the mail which, aside from the circulars, consisted of two bills, two checks, one long overdue, two inquiries that could be followed up later in the day. He had just finished and was discarding the waxed paper and cup when the outer door opened and closed. He had left his own door open, and hearing some brief exchange outside, glanced up to find Jake Kinlaw in the doorway, a cigar tucked in one corner of his thick-lipped mouth.

Kinlaw nodded, hat still on, mumbled a good morning around the cigar, and eased into the nearest chair. Fenner eyed him impatiently, annoyed somehow by such casualness.

"I thought you were supposed to take over this morning."

"Oh?" Kinlaw said, unperturbed. "I knew it was sometime today but I didn't remember setting a time. That's why I stopped by. You seen Tom yet?"

Fenner said yes, some annoyance still showing, and spoke

briefly about what had been said. "What did you find out about the regular tenants? How about the super? Have any trouble with him?"

"None. He's a wino. Name of Moretti. Has a small apartment in the building next door."

He took out a folded piece of paper and consulted some notes. What he said then gave substance to Valano's early offhand appraisals.

"First floor, two schoolteachers on one side, a married couple opposite, both work. Three airline stewardesses share one of the pads on the second; also a retired couple, the wife a semi-invalid, the husband doing the shopping and cleaning. Across from Haskell on the third another elderly couple away on a cruise."

"Good enough," Fenner said. "Now what about last night? You were out front when Haskell came in with a blond. Did either of them come out?"

"Not while I was there."

"Which was how long?"

Kinlaw seemed to hesitate. He took time to roll the cigar to the other cheek. "I'd say one-thirty, maybe a few minutes after."

"Apparently Haskell was still up there when I saw Tom earlier. I'll check with him again. You phone me here at noon and tell me where you are. I'll have Tom call and tell you where to go. Haskell's office probably."

"Fine with me."

"Now." Fenner let his chair come upright and slid forearms across the desk top. "Let's go back to last night. Anyone, not what you'd think was a regular tenant, go in or come out?"

Kinlaw took a while on that one. His glance became at once evasive and his big body fidgeted in the chair uncomfortably. When he was ready the eyes met Fenner's and he gestured emptily with one hand.

"One guy," he said, and gestured again, the hand flopping

over. "Only I sort of don't like to put a finger on him. I mean, this is strictly between us, right?"

"What else?" Fenner said bluntly. "Who's the guy and what's the problem?"

Kinlaw's glance remained steady but he took his time, his chin tilted and a slow grin beginning to twist his mouth. Removing the cigar, he said in measured words:

"The guy is Monty Saxton. The problem is I wouldn't want him to lean on me."

Fenner knew what Kinlaw meant. He had not expected the answer but having heard it and recalling the things he had learned from Kent Murdock the previous evening, he was not particularly surprised. Kinlaw seemed somewhat disappointed in the lack of reaction.

"Don't you believe me?"

"I believe you."

"You figure he called on Haskell?"

"Probably." Fenner glanced out the window, not focusing but his eyes full of thought. "Do you know anything about the local weekly high-stake poker game that's been floating around for years?"

"Not much." Kinlaw resettled the cigar in the corner of his mouth. "Only that there is one and Monty was a charter member. Why?"

"You didn't hear that Haskell had some heavy markers out?"

Kinlaw shrugged again, his tone at once disinterested. "I may have."

"What time did Saxton show?"

"Maybe eleven-thirty."

"Don't you have a watch?"

"Dashboard clock. It ain't always right."

"How long was he inside?"

"Maybe five minutes."

"How'd he get in?"

"You know the house? . . . Old brownstone. Tore down the

original entrance and ripped out the stone steps. Made the basement apartments into first-floor ones with the entrances at street level. The outer door's half glass, the inner one solid. Outer one isn't locked; mailboxes and old-time buttons and voice tubes inside."

"So?"

"Monty didn't push any buttons. I don't think he had a key but he could have. Bent over as if he was working on the keyhole. Anyway, he got in. Came back out like I say maybe four, five minutes. Looked madder'n hell."

"What makes you think so?"

"The way he took off down the street to where he'd left his car. I didn't see it, the car I mean, but old Monty was really pacing it off; kinda leaning and stiff-legged like he couldn't wait to get where he was going."

The verbal picture Kinlaw had painted seemed convincing enough but Fenner could not yet see any particular significance in it. He leaned back, gaze fixed momentarily ceilingward and his frown accentuating the angle of his brows. He nodded absently, brought his gaze back, sat straighter.

"Did you ever hear that those weekly games sometimes lasted until maybe noon the next day?"

"I don't know about that part. I understood they were usually all night affairs."

"But Saxton walked out pretty early last night."

"Maybe he was a big loser," Kinlaw said, but not emphatically; it was just something to say.

"All right. I'll stop by again and if Tom's still there I'll tell him to phone in at noon; you do the same." . . .

Tom Valano was still at ease in his car, the radio playing softly, when Fenner came alongside the lowered window just before eleven. The significance of the fact that the young photographer was still here set up a chain reaction in Fenner's thoughts that was at once vaguely disturbing.

"No action?"

"Not what you mean." Valano grinned boyishly. "But a new stewardess—I mean one I hadn't seen before—showed. Had a bag and flight kit. Must have just come in from somewhere . . . Oh, yes, and a guy," he added and described him. "I think his name is Saxton."

Fenner, about to say something, stopped with his mouth open. It took a second or two to close it but he was staring now, his eyes bright with interest.

"Monty Saxton?"

"That's the one. I heard a little about him, seen him around."

"What time?"

"Maybe a half hour ago."

"Did he get inside?"

"I guess so. He disappeared."

"How long was he there?"

"Not long. A few minutes."

Fenner thought it over speculating, not liking the situation but not knowing why. This took several seconds and by then his detective's curiosity got the best of him. Saying no more, he crossed the street, opened the outer door, glancing at the inner lock and then at the mailboxes.

He was never quite sure what made him decide to enter. At the moment there was no particular sense of foreboding that he was aware of. Possibly it was some combination of instinct and intuition that influenced him; more likely it was simply the fact that experience had taught him to be suspicious when anything in a man's habits or conduct varied from the norm.

To the best of his knowledge Mark Haskell kept normal business hours. He had been up there, at least part of the night, with some blond; he could well have a lovely hangover. But at eleven on a weekday morning? Because Fenner could not buy that, nor could he be satisfied until he found a reasonable explanation, he now considered the odds.

He was sure he could pick the lock in a few seconds but somehow he did not want to take the chance. Now, examining the name cards and seeing the three girls listed beneath apartment two-B, he pushed the button, his fingers crossed. The buzzer clicked open the inner lock almost at once and he slipped inside, heading for the nook behind the stairs. He heard the upper door open. A girl's voice said, "Yes, who is it?" and he called, "Sorry, miss, I got the wrong button."

He waited where he was until he heard the door close and the lock click in place; then went up the stairs quickly, making no sound.

There was a buzzer button recessed in the doorframe. When he had pushed it three times without response, he knocked, worrying a bit about the apartment across the hall until he remembered that this couple was on a cruise. The doors, he noticed, were probably the original ones except for the spring locks, and now, the original disturbance expanding inside him, he hesitated no longer. The little instrument, which could be classified as a burglar's tool and was highly illegal, did the job in less than twenty seconds and he stepped quickly inside, closing himself in before he glanced about.

The room was dim, the Venetian blinds slanting to cut off much of the morning light. One floor lamp was still burning and he had a vague impression of a comfortable but ordinary living room before he saw the figure on the floor and knew at once that his mental disturbance and some unacknowledged sense of foreboding had been well founded.

The sprawled still figure was perhaps six feet from the door, on its back, one arm flung wide, the other doubled under somehow so that the hand was hidden.

Identification came instantly and the only unusual aspect was that Mark Haskell was clad only in a yellow robe. It had no buttons but apparently had been belted until he had fallen. Now the belt was loose and there was a six- or eight-inch gap in front, exposing the naked body from chin to crotch, the thick chest hair darkly stained.

Aware that he had been holding his breath, Fenner let it out slowly. It took a few seconds more to realize that the faint but rhythmic pounding in his ears was his pulse. At the time he felt no great sense of shock or even surprise; rather it was some feeling of curiosity and wonderment that took over and delayed any speculation.

He had seen too many dead men—and women—some badly mutilated, to be affected in the presence of death, and it was nothing more than habit that made him kneel beside the body and touch a hand he already knew would be cold and stiff. He stayed that way only long enough to see that there were three small holes in the chest area, barely visible beneath the dried and matted blood.

He straightened then, breathing normally and no longer hearing his pulse. Avoiding any conclusion, he let his glance move the length of the living room to what looked like a small dining area. There would, he decided, be a kitchen somewhere behind it and now he focused on the hallway that opened in the right wall. Some light seemed also to come from here and he moved that way, aware that its source was a domed ceiling fixture.

The first doorway on the right gave on a good-sized bedroom with a highboy, a bureau with a wide mirror above, a chaise, and two matching boudoir chairs; an open closet was partially filled with a man's clothing.

Light still glowed from the lamp on one night table and the queen-sized bed was mussed, the covers thrown back and one pillow more indented than the other. Moving close, he saw at once the dried semen stain; then, not really thinking yet and his eyes sharply observant, he noticed the yellow hair on the pillow, not pubic but longer and straight and blond.

If he had not seen the second hair he would have let it go at that. But this second one, similar to the first, seemed caught at one end between the mattress and the headboard. For some reason, still not touching anything, he leaned close. That was how he noticed the well-hidden switch a few inches down the headboard and the tiny wire that led somewhere below.

Curiosity built swiftly and now, no longer quite so cautious, he went to his knees and peered upward from beneath the bed. When he saw the slatted wooden framework that was somehow fastened there, and the dangling wire with its little electrical clip he knew why it was there.

Almost on his belly now, he backed away and came to his knees. He stayed that way for another five seconds, thinking furiously, his angular face all humps and wrinkles. Slowly then he straightened, brushed his trousers. Finally deciding to take a chance, he carefully lifted one side of the mattress until he saw the button mike and decided that once the switch had been thrown the circuit would be activated automatically when any weight was put on the bed.

His cursory search of the room revealed nothing of interest and took no longer than a minute. It was in the living room cupboard that he found what he was looking for—an expensive, compact tape recorder and two reels of tape.

Glancing at his watch and wondering how long he had been there he put all cautionary thoughts behind him and gave in to the impulse that could no longer be resisted.

He threaded one tape, pressed the proper tab. What he heard then were the sounds of love-making, familiar to anyone who had heard and uttered them, and he was about to switch off the tape when more voices took over. It took another two or three minutes for him to understand the significance of the pillow talk that followed and the purpose behind Mark Haskell's scheme to bug himself. Then, rewinding, he put the tape back where he had found it after sliding the end through his handkerchief to wipe off any prints.

Satisfied now, he glanced round for a telephone, spotted it on a stand near the hall doorway. He was halfway to it when he stopped short, brows bunching as he considered the wisdom of making his call to Headquarters at this time. There was no thought of hindering the investigation. He hoped to get one of the two men on homicide he knew best because he felt they would like his continued cooperation.

But to phone now, to wait here, would be to admit prior entry and call for a lot more explaining than he was prepared to make. Eventually he would probably have to tell whom he was working for and why, but because he owed his clients every reasonable consideration he thought it best to give his information under more favorable and easily explained circumstances.

His choice made, he left quietly and crossed the street, trying to look nonchalant. Valano, who had been slouched lazily, camera in his lap, sat up.

"Is he up there?"

Fenner ignored the question. "What time have you got?"

Valano looked at his strapwatch. "Eight after eleven."

Fenner checked his own watch and was astonished to see that he had been away from the car less than twelve minutes.

"I'm going to give you a drill, Tom. And you damn well better remember because the police are going to ask you some questions. Once you give your story you're stuck with it. First you're going to have to tell one lie. Is it going to bother you?"

Valano sat still straighter, dark eyes wide and attentive. "Jeez, what happened up there?"

"Answer the question!"

"About lying? Will it bother me? Hell, no. You been in the army you lie pretty easy."

"When the law asks you who you're working for, and they will, you say you're working for me. You can tell them you've been watching Haskell and reporting to me but you don't know why."

"Which is the truth."

"You tell them exactly what you told me earlier. The only change is this. I stopped by first at around nine-thirty or a bit later, right? But I didn't come back until—what time did you say it was when I asked you?"

"Eight past eleven," Valano said in some bewilderment.

"And don't forget it. I came the second time at *eight after eleven.* I went over to see if I could get in because I was a bit worried and wanted to check. *Only I didn't get in because the door was locked, understand?* I came back here and told you so and asked where the nearest phone was . . . Where is it, anyway?"

"On the corner," Valano said and pointed.

"Okay," Fenner straightened. "You know all you need to know. Just get it straight the first time, Tom, and there's no sweat. If you tell it like I say, and change anything the second time around you'll be in trouble. Not as much as I will, but enough."

When Fenner talked like that you believed him and Valano, still wide-eyed but some enthusiasm beginning to show, nodded silently and Fenner started down the street. He had no trouble being connected with homicide but the detective who answered said Lieutenant Bacon had someone with him. Hoping the man might recognize his name Fenner said:

"Okay, but just break in long enough to tell him Jack Fenner's on the wire and that I say it's urgent."

The voice that finally came on was grumpy and impatient. "What is it now, Jack? What's so urgent at this time of day?"

Fenner gave the address and said: "I think there's been some trouble at the Haskell apartment on the third floor. I'm calling from the corner."

"You *think.*" Bacon's short reply sounded like a snort. "This is homicide. You think there's trouble, call the precinct."

"If that's what I thought that's what I'd do." Fenner said, his own impatience beginning to show. "My hunch says it's a lot more than that. But I'm not going to argue with you over the phone and answer four hundred silly questions." He then played his trump card. "If you don't want to be bothered switch me over to Captain Lane. Maybe he—"

"Oh, shut up!"

There was a long pause and Fenner knew why. Lane had the job that should have been Bacon's had he been somewhat more diplomatic and more willing to play politics. There was little love lost between them, and while Lane might horn in later, the thought that he, Bacon, might muff one was a little more than the lieutenant could tolerate; also he had reason to give some weight to Fenner's judgment.

"Well—" said Fenner, twisting the needle.

"All right, all right! What's that address again?"

11

They met on the sidewalk on the still sunny but chilly April morning, Jack Fenner, Lieutenant Bacon, and Sergeant Joe Gaynor, who had replaced Bacon's former assistant, Sergeant Manaham, now retired.

Bacon was a lean, straight-backed, no-nonsense veteran with a dry sense of humor and a let's-get-to-the-point approach that had ruffled a lot of feelings in the department. This morning he was, as usual, a monochrome of gray from his hat and coat to his thick gray hair and shrewd observant eyes, made more noticeable by the shaggy and much darker brows. Gaynor, much younger, his chunkiness contrasting with his superior's slatlike build, was also more affable.

He said good morning while Bacon mumbled something that came grudgingly and was less understandable. As usual he came directly to the point.

"You been up there?" he jerked a thumb at the upper floors. "No."

"How come you're here at all? What's the Haskell guy to you? Is that the Haskell that has a plant south of town somewhere?"

"We've been keeping an eye on him since yesterday afternoon—"

"Who's we?"

"Jake Kinlaw and—"

"That guy," Bacon cut in disparagingly.

"—a young fellow I don't think you know. Tom Valano. He's across the street now."

"Keeping an eye on for who?" Bacon pressed, knowing the proper usage but scorning such matters as grammar.

"I was brought in by an attorney named George Tyler," Fenner said, having no intention of mentioning Nancy Moore or Ben Clayton. "He's one of the younger partners with Esterbrook & Warren."

"The State Street law firm?" Bacon said, impressed in spite of himself.

"The same," Fenner said and grinned.

"To do what?"

"I told you, keep an eye on Haskell."

"Why?"

"Ask George Tyler."

Bacon chewed on that and decided to try another approach. "What makes you think anything is wrong upstairs?"

"He hasn't come out yet this morning."

"Maybe he's sick or something."

"He's got a telephone, hasn't he? If any doctor's been around Tom Valano didn't tell me . . . Look," Fenner added, patiently and not wanting to aggravate Bacon. "He came in last night around nine-thirty or so with a blond. Kinlaw was on until one-thirty this morning. The dame didn't come out during that time."

"Maybe they're still up there in the hay."

"Okay." Fenner spoke shortly and pretended to turn away. "You want to leave it that way, fine. I can be earning some dough instead of standing around gassing with you."

Bacon touched his arm. Fenner stopped, hiding his amusement. Bacon spoke to Gaynor.

"Push some buttons, Joe. Find the super." He surveyed the small building and the larger apartment next door. "Probably over there. Bring him, with a key." He jerked his head toward the opposite side of the street as Gaynor started off. "Let's go talk to your man. Valano, did you say? Never heard of him. In your racket, is he?"

Fenner made a quick résumé of Valano's background as they crossed the street and somewhat to his surprise Bacon dropped the mantle of blunt aggressiveness when he was introduced. He made no attempt to shake hands but nodded an acknowledgment, the gray eyes bright and observant but not hostile.

"New to the business, are you?"

"Yes, sir. I've put in for my license. I guess it's because I'm sort of good with these"—he indicated the camera in his lap with the lens that could adjust up to 300 millimeters, the reflex camera on the seat—"that I keep pretty much busy."

"I understand that you've been working for Mr. Fenner since yesterday afternoon. Keeping tabs on Mr. Haskell?"

"That's right."

"Do you know why?"

"No sir."

Bacon asked other questions but Fenner listened mostly for the answers and it was not until Valano mentioned seeing Saxton that the lieutenant interrupted, abruptly and with some stiffness.

"Saxton was here this morning? Monty Saxton?"

"I think that's his first name."

Bacon thought it over. He glanced back at the apartment building, at Fenner; then back to Valano.

"How would you know him?"

"I've seen him around. I worked about six months on the *Courier* for Kent Murdock."

Bacon asked about Haskell's movements the night before and now he turned back to Fenner, gaze slightly narrowed and mildly suspicious.

"What bugs me," he said, "is why Haskell's getting all this attention. Some divorce business maybe?"

"You'll have to ask—"

"I know, I know. You say this Esterbrook & Warren's guy is

named Tyler? Okay. But I get the idea that you think something might happen to Haskell, like something violent maybe. What makes you think so, or don't you?"

"Because with a character like Haskell—and you'll find out why soon enough if you want to check—there's always a chance of trouble. If you want specifics ask George Tyler."

Bacon didn't like it but a whistle from Sergeant Gaynor across the street forestalled further comment. He was standing near the entrance alongside a short, round-bodied man in slacks and a sweater. When Bacon glanced up and down the street to see if it was safe to cross, Fenner whispered: "Nice going," to Valano and followed the lieutenant.

Jake Kinlaw's description of the super, Frank Moretti, as a wino, was confirmed by his coloring, his blue-veined nose, and his breath. The sweater was out at the elbows and his felt hat was grimy and stained, but he was cheerful enough when Bacon, flashing his shield, told him what he wanted.

"Certainly, Lieutenant." He bowed and made a sweeping gesture. "This way."

They went inside and up the stairs in single file, the super leading and Fenner bringing up the rear. At Haskell's door the super selected a key from a large bunch but Bacon motioned that *he* wanted it. Gaynor was already knocking and after a decent interval Bacon turned the lock, took a half step to peer inside. Stopping right there he spoke over his shoulder to Moretti, returning the keys and telling him to go back to his quarters and wait.

"The sergeant will be along in a few minutes. He'll want to talk to you, understand."

"Something has happened to Mr. Haskell?"

"We'll let you know later."

He waited until the super turned away, cocked his head at Fenner, and said: "Quite a hunch you had, Jackson, quite a hunch."

Fenner was the last one in and he whistled softly and said:

"Wow!" to show he was surprised. Bacon merely touched one wrist of the body and told Gaynor to get the blinds.

Light from the two windows made everything starkly clear now, giving to the half-naked form a sort of waxen repulsiveness that was shocking to see. Bacon, having made a slow circuit, went to one knee, his interest caught by the hand that had been twisted beneath the body. He rolled it just enough to get a peek, then let the form roll back.

"Got a gun in his hand," he said, half to himself. "We'll leave it for the medical examiner. Don't want any static from his office."

He stood up, scratched behind one ear, pushed his hat back from his forehead. He unbuttoned his topcoat and fanned back the tails, standing there immobile, hands on hips until Gaynor, who had disappeared, called from the hall.

"Hey, Lieutenant. In here."

Fenner tagged along, in no hurry. By the time he reached the bedroom both men were bent over the bed, their eyes probing and intent. Presently Gaynor spotted one of the hairs as Fenner knew he would. He pointed and Bacon grunted.

"Leave it for the lab boys. Unless we find her and get a sample of her hair all they'll be able to tell us anyway is that it's human hair."

Gaynor said: "Here's another one," and then he was going through the same movement Fenner had made.

Because he knew what would happen he turned his thoughts inward to speculate once more why Mark Haskell had rigged such a device. Since he knew more than Bacon did at the moment it was logical to assume that the blond was Monty Saxton's Sandra Joslin. If this were so then he could begin to understand something of the pillow talk he had heard on the tape. He waited patiently, saying nothing to distract the detectives until they too had located the recorder and the two tapes in the living room cupboard.

He watched Gaynor thread one of them and press the proper tab and then they were listening.

First there came a smothered expletive, a man's chuckle, some giggles, sighs . . . Silence and the faint suggestion of some movement that one could imagine developed a rhythm . . . Heavy breathing, now faster until everything was quiet and the man said: "All right, baby?" and the girl said: "Oh, yesss, honey. You know it was."

Fenner had seldom seen Bacon embarrassed but it showed now in the high color, the averted gaze. He had not moved in thirty seconds and he continued to stand there when the talk began again.

The girl said: "I'll have one too, please." A match scratched and you could hear it blown out. Then they were talking, the man asking questions, the girl answering. Some of these questions and answers were revealing but, oddly, no names mentioned. Some third male was referred to as *he* or the *boyfriend*. Only once was there a name and that was: *Sylvia*. After several minutes, complete silence came and Gaynor switched off the machine.

Bacon exhaled noisily, lips pushing in and out a moment before he remembered why he was here. He looked at Fenner, chin tipping and the gray eyes probing.

"What do *you* make of it?"

"Same as you. A guy and a girl making love."

"And all that chatter afterward?"

"Sounds as if the man might want a bit of blackmail material. Some of the answers could be called classified."

Bacon chewed on this a moment, offering no argument. He seemed to be listening to Sergeant Gaynor who was talking on the telephone. Presently he waved at a chair.

"Sit down, Jack. While we're waiting for the M.E. let's talk some more, hunh?"

He waited until Fenner took a chair by the window, then sat himself on the edge of a couch.

"If I remember right you were supposed to have one of the best ears in the business for voices, even on the telephone or a recording."

"I'm pretty good on smells too."

Bacon glared but kept his temper. "Just stick to voices, hunh?"

Fenner nodded, knowing that what the lieutenant said was true. He could identify singers and orchestras when most people failed. Even bands and singers going back twenty years provided they were once popular. Most well-known instrumentalists too. Tuning in on the middle of a record he could identify individuals by the style, the technique, the tone, the phrasing —except lately when all the singers, both male and female, seemed intent on either whining nasally or shouting, or in some way they thought dramatic, warping completely both lyrics and music. The same applied to all the groups with funny names, and five guitars and a bass, who played three-chord pieces, the melody, if any, too repetitious to bear. To him they all sounded alike. He knew it dated him but he still preferred Ella and Maxine and Peggy, who not only could stick with the melody but made you feel and understand the lyrics . . .

"What?" he said.

"Pay attention!" Bacon said. "We can assume the guy on the recording is this Haskell you were interested in but could you identify his voice?"

"Sure."

"Is that a guess?"

"No. I talked to him in his office yesterday afternoon."

"Oh? How come?"

"I'd seen him around. I wanted a closer look. And you know something? Close up he reminded me of a satyr. And a satyr is supposed to be lascivious, and Haskell, from what I've heard, sure as hell was."

"Oh, shut up. You and your education . . . How about the dame?"

Fenner had a good idea about her too because of what Murdock had told him and what he had learned from Fred Glover's report.

"Is there any *quid pro quo* in this?"

"What the hell is *quid pro quo?*"

"It's going to get around that old Jack Fenner, one of the best in the business, was supposed to be watching a guy when someone butts in and knocks him off." He tipped one hand and let it drop. He grinned crookedly. "It doesn't look good."

"Come on, come on."

"If I cooperate, and I don't have to beyond a point, will you level with me when I want something from you?"

"Like what?"

"Information. Progress."

"Probably. Like you said, to a point. So answer my question."

"I never heard that voice," Fenner said, pleased that he did not yet have to lie.

"Have you got any ideas about that blond?"

"One. Strictly rumor." He digressed to speak of his conversation with Kent Murdock. "Monty Saxton is said to have some doll tucked away here in town. Brought her up from New Orleans. She doesn't get around much but she has been seen at the track and at hockey games. Freezes any attempt at a pick up. On rare occasions she's been seen with Saxton; maybe a couple of times with Mark Haskell."

"Does she have a name?"

"Murdock might know," Fenner said casually, hoping the evasion would go unnoticed.

"You know where she lives?"

"No." The lie came easily.

"Haskell was married, right? You know anything about the marriage?"

"Haskell has a home in Dedham. I understand he and his wife were separated."

Bacon's eyes had drifted and he spoke more to himself than Fenner.

"A jealous wife could do a job like this. Catch the husband red-handed. When he opens the door let him have three quick ones. He must have been a little jumpy or he wouldn't have come to the door with a gun, maybe in the robe pocket. Only he wasn't quick enough with it . . . Jake Kinlaw was on last night?"

"Until one-thirty or so; at least that's what he told me."

"You've seen him this morning?"

"In my office. He stopped by to give his report. He saw Haskell and the blond come in around nine-thirty. So did Valano. He didn't see her come out."

"Could she have been here when Haskell got it?"

"Maybe when the M.E. gives us an idea of the time of death—"

"Sure, sure. So skip the conjecture. Did Kinlaw see anyone else that maybe wasn't a tenant?"

"One man."

Bacon sat up. "Who?"

"You're going to question Kinlaw?"

"You're damn right we'll question him."

"Then why not let him tell you?"

"Because, if you want that *quid pro quo*," he said dryly, "maybe we can save some time."

"Monty Saxton."

Bacon leaned forward from the waist, the eyes open and mildly incredulous. "The hell you say! Last night, and again this morning, hunh? What's the rest of it?"

Fenner repeated the things Kinlaw had told him. Bacon nodded, a glint of satisfaction showing.

"Up here maybe five minutes. Plenty of time. Maybe the right time."

"If he did the job, why come back this morning?"

"Who knows?"

Bacon moved back to the body and stood staring at it but touching nothing. This gave Fenner a chance to do some thinking, and so absorbed did he become in his mental review that he did not realize Bacon was talking to him until he glanced up and found the gray gaze boring into him.

"What did you say?"

"I said, 'Some hunch you had.' "

"What hunch?" Fenner said defensively.

"Coming up here to find a guy with three slugs in the chest, a guy you were supposed to be watching—for some reason we intend to discover one way or another."

"Lay off. You know I—"

"You were awfully damn anxious for us to come up here and take a look. Why? Come on, come clean!"

"Cut it out!" Fenner was no longer amused and he was bothered by the lieutenant's astuteness even though he knew it was only a shot in the dark. "I told you why I was suspicious. I found out some things since yesterday morning."

"Like?"

"I told you that too. Haskell was trouble. He gave it, made it, thrived on it. You'll find out when you start digging."

"Sure I will," Bacon said without much conviction. "But what I want to know now is why would someone pay you and two other guys fat prices to watch Haskell. You can be made to tell, you know."

Fenner shook his head, amusement once more glinting from the green eyes. He took his time answering. Then, with a schoolmaster's pedantic manner, and giving Bacon his Mephistophelian look, he said:

"We've been over this before, Lieutenant. You know I can be made to tell, I know it. But unless you can lay the obstructing bit on me later, I don't have to talk now or even in your office. You can take me down and I'll phone my attorney and be out in ten minutes and the D.A.'ll laugh at you. I have no legal privilege, true, but—"

"Ahh," Bacon said disgustedly. "You and your legal training. Why the hell didn't you finish up and get your degree?"

"The lure of the uniform and the fat pension was too great."

"Yeah, yeah, yeah," Bacon said, trying to sound indignant while his sense of humor got the best of him. "So why didn't you stick it out? From what I heard you were doing okay."

Fenner had a ready answer but he held it while his mind went back. He had known Bacon only slightly when he had been with the department. Bacon had been a sergeant then, recently appointed to homicide, and Fenner had seldom had much to do with that branch. When he had worked, as a precinct detective, on a murder, it was only because he had been the one to answer the original call. In such cases it was mostly a matter of cooperation, with everyone pitching in and covering assigned areas.

But even then he had known the lieutenant's reputation for competence and dedication to the job. Since he, Fenner, had been on his own he had been able on some occasions to offer a bit of useful information. He needed the cooperation from friends and acquaintances from time to time. It made his own job easier and he tried to repay the favors when he could. Now wanting to show his good will, but at the same time aware of his obligation to his clients, he felt he was doing the right thing at the moment. Satisfied, he answered Bacon's question.

"Because," he said, and he was no longer kidding, "the courts from the Supreme on down made it damn near impossible to do my job. And crummy lawyers screaming for publicity and the rights of everyone but the victim, and the stays, and postponements and red tape; yes, judges too, until your witness disappeared or lost his memory, and the bastard you know is guilty walking out and laughing in your face because of a mistrial or a hung jury or some silly technicality."

Bacon said: "Sure, Jack," but Fenner hadn't finished.

"I saw some figures the other day. Some syndicated columnist. I know those guys aren't always accurate, but he must have got his statistics somewhere. In New York City last year the police made some ninety thousand felony arrests. You want to know how many went to trial? Five hundred and twenty-two . . . With you, a family man, and only a few years from a nice thirty-year pension, it makes some sense maybe to stick it out —and someone has to. With me, I say the hell with it."

That was a lot of talk for Fenner and he meant every word of it. The effect was to sober the lieutenant, and the look of resignation in the gray eyes suggested that he concurred.

"Okay, the hell with it. I'm sorry I asked."

As he spoke the medical examiner's deputy came in, a neat slender man with a mustache and dark-rimmed glasses. By the time he had started to examine the body, two technical men came in with their gear followed presently by a precinct plain-clothesman and a uniformed lieutenant, also from the precinct.

They went into a huddle off to one side but what they were saying held no interest for Fenner and he watched the doctor testing wrists, neck, and legs, all of which, from where Fenner stood, seemed quite stiff and immobile. In less than two minutes the doctor rose, picked up the unopened black bag, and spoke to the group at one side.

"Nothing more for me," he said. "You can go ahead. The ambulance boys are outside when you're ready." He indicated the gun, now in plain sight. "I haven't touched this."

One of the tech men said: "Won't be a lousy print on it anyway. Never yet found one worth a damn." And his companion said: "How right you are. But we still have to give it a try."

Bacon, stepping away from the huddle as the doctor reached the door, said: "When, Doc? Approximately."

"It's always approximate at this stage. Possibly between one and three this morning. Instantaneous, or nearly so."

Fenner got a cigarette going and went back to the chair by the window, ignoring the routine he had seen too many times. He knew when Bacon was ready he'd be back, and he was somewhat concerned as to how long he could keep Ben Clayton and Nancy Moore out of this. He knew either Bacon or one of his men would go see George Tyler, and since both Clayton and the girl were bona fide clients Tyler did not have to tell the police much.

For all of this, once Bacon started digging, he was going to find some connection between Haskell and the others involved. The Haskell Company takeover business would certainly become known and considered as a factor. Marion Haskell could not long remain hidden. George Tyler was unlikely to hinder a legitimate police investigation deliberately and only should an arrest of one of his clients be imminent could he claim privilege. Perhaps the most important and immediate thing now was to let Ben Clayton know what had happened and what to expect.

He was not sure how long he sat there, conscious of little but his own problems. Only when he finally looked up and realized Bacon was standing in front with more questions did he sense that except for him and the lieutenant only the technical men were left.

"Know where we can locate this Mrs. Haskell?" Bacon was saying. "Joe Gaynor phoned the Haskell residence. She hasn't been there for several days."

"No." Fenner said, not liking the lie but wanting this information to come from Clayton. For there was no way Ben Clayton could be long kept out of this. Bacon would learn of the prior marriage; he would discover why it had gone on the rocks. When he got into the family business and Mark Haskell's will, if any, and heirs, he would have to learn about Nancy Moore. He would naturally question all of them and he was certain to uncover Haskell's threats and near-psychotic behavior. He would also eventually consider everyone involved as potential suspects. Now, because it seemed pointless to be obstinate, Fenner said:

"Her name is Marion. I mean Mrs. Haskell. She used to be married to Ben Clayton."

"Who's he?"

"Executive vice-president of Haskell & Company."

"They have an office in town?"

Fenner supplied the address and Bacon made a note. He then turned to Sergeant Gaynor who had wandered in.

"Joe." He gave him the note. "Check on this guy. Friend of Haskell's and once married to the present Mrs. Haskell."

When Gaynor left Bacon began to button his coat. He straightened his hat, then rocked a few times, heel and toe, head cocked as he surveyed Fenner.

"I'm going to leave the tech men"—he turned and told one

of them to be sure and take the tapes and recorder—"and pay a call. It's time I had a talk with a guy."

Fenner thought he knew what the lieutenant had in mind but understood he was expected to comment. "Who?"

"Monty Saxton. If you want some of the *quid pro quo* you can tag along. You can ride with me."

"Un-unh."

Bacon's surprise showed at the quick refusal and Fenner hurried to explain.

"Oh, I want to go all right," he said, "but I have to tell Tom Valano he's through and call Kinlaw—"

"And tell him to stay available."

"—and I have to call my office. I'll meet you wherever you say."

"Where do you think we'll find old Monty?"

The question was chiefly rhetorical since Bacon knew as well as anyone where Saxton's headquarters were.

They left together, Bacon leading, and the press was waiting on the sidewalk—three reporters and two photographers but no one from the TV stations. Fortunately for Fenner they directed their attack at Bacon. For it had become his practice since he had been on his own to avoid any such publicity. Two basic reasons prompted such conduct—he did not want to become known to the public, as such, and perhaps more important, he had learned that police officers were often annoyed at any publicity not directed at members of the fraternity. Fenner knew well no more than three newspapermen and he wanted to keep it that way.

Now with Bacon besieged, he was able to detour and cross the street more or less unnoticed. Valano, who had seen the coming and going of official cars and the ambulance, was waiting, eyes wide with curiosity and anticipation.

"It was a short assignment, Tom," Fenner said, "but bill me for a full day."

"But what the hell happened?"

"Our man got himself shot last night after Kinlaw left."

"Haskell? Jesus, what do you know? So what about the blond I saw go in with him?"

"Missing. Must have blown some time after Kinlaw called it off. I have to make some phone calls at that corner booth. I'll need a lift downtown because I think it's best to leave my car here and pick it up later. I'll tell you about it on the way. When you get a chance, phone Kinlaw. Tell him what happened and that he'll be getting a visit from Lieutenant Bacon or one of his men."

12

Ben Clayton's line was busy when Fenner got the Haskell Company office but he asked the girl to cut in and tell Clayton who was calling and that it was a matter of the utmost importance. When Clayton finally answered he spent no time on preliminaries.

"You sitting down? Well Haskell won't be killing anybody now because somebody took care of him last night between one and three."

He heard the startled, incredulous exclamation but went on to give the necessary details in short clipped phrases, adding: "I thought I'd warn you that there's no way you can avoid questioning and my advice is to level with Lieutenant Bacon or Sergeant Gaynor or whoever wants to see you."

Clayton said just one understandable word after Fenner's first announcement: *God!* Now there was only the sound of heavy breathing and Fenner waited until the voice, choked with worry and concern, said:

"Have you told the police about me?"

"Not that I was working for you or why. But George Tyler will probably have to. They are going to get to you one way or the other and the more evasive you are the more suspicious they'll be."

"Then you didn't tell them I was with you last night?"

"We didn't get that far. Just tell the truth and I'll back you up."

"But, my God, Jack—" The voice sounded sick with dismay. "I mean, you don't have to tell them about all those drunken threats I made last night. I was going to phone you later and apologize for being such an ass and to thank you for getting me sloshed enough so I could sleep it off . . . Jesus!" he breathed. "If I have to tell them about those threats—"

"Look," Fenner said, trying not to sound impatient, "if you tell the police you spent the night with me they're going to want to know why you came there in the first place. They're going to find out why I was working for you. They'll know we weren't buddies. So eventually they are going to have to be told that you got plastered and had this silly idea and stopped by with the wild idea of getting to Haskell first. I can give you an alibi and I will but I'm afraid that won't be enough. I think it might be better if that information came from you first because I'll sure as hell have to tell the truth eventually if they press me hard enough. Talk to Tyler if you want. He's your attorney. You'll have to level with him."

"All right." The voice was barely audible. "But—I mean, just suppose I hadn't come there? Suppose I'd stayed home and couldn't prove it?"

"I have to run." Fenner broke it off, his tone flat and incisive. "Think it over. Do as you like but you can only count on me up to a point. Quit supposing and relax. If George Tyler doesn't bring you into it I'll probably have to. I thought I should tell you. I have some friends in the department; I want to keep them."

When he had called his office and told Alice Maxwell he didn't know where he'd be but would call back, he went to Valano's sporty hardtop and told him where he wanted to be dropped . . .

The office of Tri-State Loan was well down Washington Street, a narrow-front place with the company name and business lettered on the plate-glass window. Bacon was already there, holding up the corner of the building, and he mumbled some complaints about Fenner's tardiness before he turned into the entrance.

The longish front room was typical. Three girls sat at typewriter desks on the right, with a glassed-in cashier's quarters beyond them, while opposite were four desks, each with a waist-high partition separating them. Wooden name markers stood at the corners to let the potential customer know whom he was dealing with. Two interviewers had customers. One desk had no occupant at the moment and the Mr. Eiserberg— so the nameplate said—at the fourth was doing some paper work. All were in their thirties, very neat and efficient-looking in business suits, not a longhair among them.

As Fenner followed Bacon down the aisle toward the closed wooden door at the end he reviewed his knowledge about the operation. The front office was strictly legitimate, complying to the letter of the law about interest rates and procedures. However, the back room was said to deal in larger sums, the loans often made on collateral that banks thought inadequate, but bearing rates of interest that were often confiscatory and could force an unwary businessman into a situation where Saxton and associates could wind up owning a major interest.

It was said that this was how Saxton became the owner of a linen supply business that had as customers most of the city's bars and restaurants; the laundry that did the work had been acquired in somewhat the same manner. There were also tales, none yet proved, of some violence as well as pressures of one sort or another on delinquent borrowers and their families.

Beyond the cashier there was a fenced-off space presided over by a tinted blond with a noteworthy figure.

"Yes?" she said with her practiced empty smile.

"Mr. Saxton in?" Bacon said.

"May I ask who's calling?"

"You may. Lieutenant Bacon, city police. Is he in?"

"Well—he has someone with him—"

"That's all right," Bacon said, reaching for the knob. "You don't have to announce us."

Fenner eyed her confusion with amusement as the painted mouth opened to protest while the impulse died in her shadowed eyes.

Saxton's office was impressive, not large but expensively furnished, the carpet thick and spotless, the leather divan at least eight feet long, the three matching chairs deep-cushioned. The leather-backed chair behind the executive's handsome desk was four inches higher than Saxton's sleek head and there was a flash of quick displeasure when the door opened and he saw his visitors.

The blond young man who had been bending over one end of the desk straightened. He was built like a defensive tackle and had an athlete's rugged good looks. Now he frowned uncertainly, taking a quick glance at his employer for some clue as to the reaction expected. He settled for a protective stance behind and slightly to the right of the chair.

Bacon looked round approvingly, unbuttoned his coat and gave Saxton a thin mirthless smile before he settled himself on the divan and said: "Good morning, Monty."

Saxton did not like it. The tight lips beneath the small black mustache said so. Scowling, brows twisted, he waited for Bacon to speak but the lieutenant outwaited him, the thin grin constant and gray gaze fixed. After maybe fifteen seconds of this while the look of puzzlement on the blond man's face expanded Saxton gave in.

"All right, Lieutenant. What do you want?"

"A little conversation . . . You know Jack Fenner, don't you? He's also interested in the matter we're going to discuss."

"What matter?"

"The killing early this morning, by three slugs in the chest, of a friend of yours."

Nothing changed in Saxton's face. When he was ready he said: "Has this guy got a name?"

"Mark Haskell."

"Haskell. A friend? Who gave you that idea?"

"You don't know him?"

"Just barely. Like to say hello."

"A little better than that, Monty. He was a regular in your weekly poker game, at least until recently."

"All right."

"I also heard he was a regular contributor with markers here and there, and that you bought up these markers at a discount to get the leverage you wanted."

Fenner listened with mounting interest because he always liked to see Bacon work—on other people. He did not even wonder where the lieutenant got his information, because it was Bacon's job to know about anything that might one day concern him, all of which was duly filed in his memory bank.

Now, as the lieutenant continued, Fenner used his own memory bank to review what he knew about Saxton's past.

Never associated with the Mafia, but of late apparently having some working agreement with the local members, Saxton had as a young man been known as a mobster and a member of an Irish group which, considering the ethnic breakdown of the city, was not surprising. His rap sheet showed early arrests for assault and extortion. Twice he was brought in on suspicion of murder, but his single conviction had resulted in a suspended sentence and a short period of probation.

Some years back a vendetta had split the Irish mob—over a girl it was said—and like some early Cosa Nostra families they started knocking each other off. On street corners, and getting off buses, and in the backs of cars, frequently right out in the open with no regard for witnesses or the man in the street. Saxton, having no basic Irish affiliation, wisely left town for a while. But being a smart and efficient operator by that time he had found an opening wedge here and there, not hesitating to use muscle, or hire it, but staying away from dope and prostitution and the numbers to avoid conflict with those more strongly entrenched.

Gambling, some modest bookmaking, and the loan business

had been the cornerstone of his prosperity, and in addition to the profitable Tri-State Loan, and the linen service, he was said to own a couple of business buildings. He had also financed, for a percentage, a noted diamond fence, a licensed dealer never arrested. Some of the wares he sold and traded with the New York operators were rumored to have come from the breakup of jewelry stolen in several spectacular East Coast burglaries from Boston to Miami.

This mental review took no more than ten seconds and now Fenner was listening again as Bacon probed and prodded and Saxton said in sarcastic challenging tones:

"Look, Lieutenant, if this is a pinch you ought to be telling me my rights, hadn't you?"

"No pinch, Monty," Bacon said in even tones. "Like I said, just some conversation. And if you think your poker-playing friends are going to alibi you, think again. Maybe some. But we know the regulars and I think a couple might rather talk than have us open the books on a few things we've been letting simmer until we needed an edge.

"Also we have the word of one of Fenner's men that you visited Haskell's apartment last night around eleven-thirty and were upstairs five minutes. He's an ex-cop named Jake Kinlaw, and he has no reason to lie. Also from here it looked like a professional hit. Haskell opens the door and that's it, right from the hall."

Saxton leaned back in his chair and his black eyes took on a sleepy look.

Bacon said: "You were also seen going there this morning. So I've been wondering. Last night was Tuesday. Poker night. But you leave early. Maybe to talk to Haskell about the markers. Maybe because you found out, or suspected, that the blond doll you imported from New Orleans a few months back had been cheating on you with Haskell those Tuesday nights.

"A dame like that shouldn't take us too long to run down. Even Jack here knows about her," Bacon added, not expecting a reply. "The way we see it, it's even possible she might have been in the bedroom. We're pretty sure they were in the sack and had had their fun before the gun came. Did you know Haskell had bugged his bed with a pressure contact?"

Saxton's eyes remained sleepy but things were happening behind them. His colorless face was set and tight-lipped. Bacon turned his gaze on the oversized youth but spoke to Saxton.

"You want sonny to hear the details or do you want him to take the air a few minutes?"

Saxton, glancing over his shoulder, seemed to have forgotten his aide. Now he jerked his chin at a door in the back wall that led to his private parking lot. The blond went through it and closed the door softly.

"I'm going to tell you a little of what was on those tapes," Bacon said, and did so. When he finished he added: "The way it looked to me this Haskell was not only humping your broad but pumping her when he was through, like where she came from and what she was getting a month for keeping herself available for daddy.

"The reason I know about her is, like I said, Jack Fenner here, who was also interested in her. Seems he picked up a couple of rumors from Kent Murdock of the *Courier*. Because the girl— and I understand she's got the kind of build you notice—has been seen around, mostly alone, but a couple of times with you; a couple other times in out-of-the-way restaurants having dinner with Haskell. No nightclubbing, just restaurants. Funny too," he said sardonically, "but no names were mentioned on the tape—except one. A woman, name of Sylvia . . . For the record Monty, what's your wife's name?"

That was the end. Fenner knew it and so did Bacon. Saxton jerked out of the chair and stood stiffly, jaw jutting and his face livid, fists opening and closing convulsively at his sides.

"Get out of here you bastard! You want to talk to me again, you take me in, you stinking bastard!"

Bacon stood up and started to rebutton his coat, nothing

showing on his lean weathered face. He gave Fenner a slow wink and waved toward the door.

"Whatever you say, Monty. If and when we take you in I'll read your rights. But if you're smart I'd call my shyster now. Tell him to keep available. If he's out of town tell him to get back here and stand by. Because I have an idea you're going to need him. We've only been on this a little over an hour and look how far we are already." He looked around, nodded approvingly. "Nice place you've got here," he added as he went out.

On the sidewalk Bacon stopped at the curb away from the busy pedestrian flow. "He could be made to fit," he said thoughtfully. "He had Haskell in hock and Haskell used the girl once a week. He pumps her in bed—and I don't mean that the way it sounds—so what happens if Saxton's wife gets a listen at those tapes?" He peered slantingly at Fenner. "Do you know if her name is Sylvia?"

"I think so, I think Murdock mentioned the name. I know I've seen her with Saxton—shortish, a bit plump but smart-looking."

"And from what I hear"—Bacon was nodding to himself now as he developed the thought—"most of what Saxton owns is in his wife's name, maybe through dummies, maybe not . . . What do you think?"

"An interesting premise except—"

"Except what?"

"If the examiner's man is right, Saxton had been there and left sometime before the shooting."

Bacon shook off the objection. "He went there and couldn't get in—remember he must have tumbled or been tipped off to where the girl was—and that made him flip. So he went back later with a gun. He was an enforcer years ago, up twice on suspicion of murder—"

"But not lately. If he wanted to put Haskell away he'd fly in a button man."

"Maybe, but this was no business thing," Bacon argued. "This was personal. If he was mad enough he could have done it himself . . . Well, I'll talk to Kinlaw and see if we can locate Haskell's wife. It could still shape up that way, with the wife doing the job I mean. Happened that way more times than you can remember. Still does. Read the papers . . . You want a lift?"

"Yes. Back to Haskell's place. Valano dropped me off here."

13

It was nearly two when Jack Fenner returned to his office, and Alice Maxwell was not yet back from her lunch. When he had unlocked the door and moved on into his private office he saw the two telephone slips on his desk. Both said that Mr. Clayton had phoned. The times were noted with the added penciled comment: I didn't know where to tell him you were.

When he returned the call and was told by the Haskell operator that Mr. Clayton would not be back for another half hour, he slipped out of his Shetland jacket, loosened his tie, and thought of the Bourbon bottle in the lower drawer of his desk. He did not want a drink just for the sake of a drink but knew a prelunch drop would whet his appetite.

The green metal carafe that had been filled with coffee earlier would, he knew, now have cold water which Alice got from the cooler in the outer office; the two glasses sparkled because she kept a small box of soap powder in her desk. The very thought of losing such a girl to her young intern depressed him momentarily, and then, shaking off the thought, he reached for the telephone and dialed a delicatessen halfway down the side street, asking for Eddie.

"Jack Fenner, Eddie."

"Yes, Mr. Fenner. How're things today?"

"What's good?"

"How would some corned beef strike you, fresh this morning."

Fenner said it would strike him fine. "On rye, Eddie. Mustard on the side. A double coffee, light. But not so damn light it's lukewarm when you get here."

"Gotcha, Mr. Fenner. On the way."

Aware that on the way meant ten or twelve minutes, Fenner reached for the proper drawer and splashed an inch of whisky into the glass, adding cold water from the carafe. He got a cigarette going and leaned back, his gaze reflective and ceiling-ward as he felt the pleasant warmth of the whisky in his gullet.

He was on his last swallow when Eddie came bustling in and marched up to the desk, his freckled grin broad and genuine. He was no drop-the-bag-and-run youngster either. He opened the bag, removed a small paper plate he had included, unwrapped the waxed paper carefully and placed the two fat halves of the sandwich on the plate. He took the top off the coffee container and brought forth a tiny paper cup with its own top.

"Your mustard, Mr. Fenner. I figured you could use the paper coffee spoon to spread it."

Eddie gave such service because he knew Fenner was a good tipper and he was not disappointed this time. His smile said so as he saluted and withdrew . . .

Fenner was on the last of his coffee when Alice came in, shucked off her coat, fluffed her hair, and deposited her bag in a desk drawer. She asked if Fenner had reached Mr. Clayton. He said no, and would she try again. She went out, closing his door behind her. Presently his phone rang and Ben Clayton's voice came to him.

"I phoned George Tyler after I talked to you this morning," Clayton said, his voice noticeably nervous and agitated. "Tyler called me back later. He said someone from the police had asked to see him and he made a date for two. I told him that you were there when they found Mark and that you had to tell them that George had hired you. He said that was all right and that he would probably have to tell whoever saw him why he called you in and what I wanted you to do.

"He came right out and asked me point blank whether I had anything to do with it and I said I spent the night at your place because I got drunk. He said in that case I should answer the detective's questions, tell the truth. So I'm expecting somebody will be dropping in almost any time."

Fenner said he thought Tyler's advice was sound. "It's a Lieutenant Bacon's case at the moment. He's a good man. If he doesn't come it will probably be his sidekick, a Sergeant Gaynor. Before the police finish they're going to find out about Haskell's threats and they'll not only question you but Nancy Moore and her actor boyfriend. What Bacon really wants is to find Marion Haskell. Have you talked to her?"

"Not yet. I didn't know what to say or how to say it."

"She ought to know, and the sooner the better. The police are going to get to her eventually and she ought to be ready because they are likely to bear down a bit."

"But why? She couldn't have had anything to do with it."

"That she may have to prove. Because when a husband gets knocked off that way the wife, unless there are witnesses that say otherwise, is the number-one suspect. A marriage on the rocks, a jealous wife, a cheating husband—"

"God!" Clayton said, his voice barely audible. "I never thought of that." He paused and when he continued his words were indignant. "But that's absurd, Jack."

"Not to the police. Do you think she's been sticking pretty much to that apartment?"

"I told her to. I said to stay in the neighborhood."

"Let me ask you something. Did you know about Haskell and the weekly poker games they have around town?"

"Yes. He's been doing that for some time."

"Did you know he was a heavy loser?"

"Not really. I did find out that he put up some of his company stock for some sort of loan not too long ago. I don't know who made the loan. It got around somehow here in the office and I wondered why he needed that kind of cash."

"Does the name Monty Saxton mean anything to you?"

"I seem to have heard it, or maybe seen it in the papers. Why? Who is he?"

"An ex-mobster. Has some legitimate businesses nowadays, principally a loan office."

He went on to explain the situation and Saxton's possible motive and connection with the murder. Then aware that he was digressing to no worthwhile purpose he came back to the main issue.

"What about Marion Haskell?"

"I don't know, Jack . . . I mean, I'd hate to tell her over the phone, and I can't very well go out there now. Do you think the police might have someone following me or anything like that?"

"Offhand, no. Would you like me to tell her?"

"Would you—until I get a chance to see her myself? . . . Just a minute . . . The girl says someone from the police is here now. I'd better ring off."

Fenner leaned back in his chair, replacing the handset carefully, his frown warping the corners of his eyes. Presently, out of nowhere, another thought came and he swore under his breath, his irritation directed at himself and his lapse of memory. Swiveling, he lifted the phone again and reached for his ever-present notebook.

"Alice. I want a West Coast number. A Mr. Johnson." He read off the number. "If he's not in find out from his secretary or answering service when he's expected back."

He hung up again, the scowl constant as he translated the hour into Pacific time. He sat that way for perhaps three minutes and then the phone buzzed.

"Mr. Johnson stepped out. He's expected back within a half hour. I left our number. Will he know what it's about?"

Fenner said yes, that he had phoned Johnson the day before. Then he sat back to wait, trying to concentrate on some paper work, figuring how much Kinlaw and Tom Valano would have coming for their time, and his cut. He also tried to estimate his own working time on the case in addition to the hour or so he had given Esterbrook & Warren.

The half-hour delay turned out to be considerably more than that and it was after three when Johnson returned his call.

"Jack? Sorry I was out. Something came up that took longer than I expected."

"My fault," Fenner said. "I couldn't phone when I said I would because I was with the law. A guy we had been watching got himself shot in his apartment sometime last night. I was with the police when they found the body this morning."

"Sounds like fun. Maybe I should move East and get in on some of that."

"Just give me your flight number and I'll be at the airport to meet you."

"Anything to do with our friend Barry Wilbur? I mean this shooting?"

"It's possible—the police haven't questioned him yet—but I sort of doubt it. Did you have any luck?"

"Nothing startling because there wasn't much to this one. You gave me most of it beforehand. Registered with all the actors' guilds. Worked fairly steadily, has a small bungalow up in the hills. Came here three years ago from Kansas City by way of New York—some actors' workshop training. Thirty-one years old; married but separated. Apparently did all right with the girls."

"Any record?"

"Nothing serious. Picked up once by the Beverly police as a prowler. The dame that complained said it was a mistake. Aside from some traffic tickets, two simple assaults. One nol-prossed; drew a fine and a warning on the second. But he does have the reputation of being a hothead.

"Now this Nancy Moore"—a pause as if to consult some notes —"no trouble with the law. Worked for more than a year in one of the local barber shops like you said. Nothing unusual until a couple guys show up a while back. Something about being a missing heir. Anything to that?"

"Only that it happens to be true. She's now here to claim her share under her real father's will. Had a little trouble from the guy who got shot last night—he was her half-brother—and Wilbur flew East to be with her. I talked to him. Seemed okay but the damn fool admitted he had a gun. The police, when they get to him, may give him a little heat on that. Anything else on the girl?"

"Mother thought to have died two or three years ago. The girl married once to a stock-car racer who got himself killed. Twenty-seven. No trouble. Had plenty of boyfriends. Period. Ten-four. Et cetera, et cetera."

Fenner laughed, thanked Johnson again, said to send the tab along, and hung up . . .

Not until Jack Fenner had started for Marion Haskell's place did it occur to him that there was another necessary stop that he should make en route. It would not take long and he knew it was time Nancy Moore learned what had happened last night and got ready for some eventual police interrogation.

He had never been in this particular apartment house before. He recalled that she said she had rented the place furnished and his first glimpse over her shoulder into the living room when she opened the door would have suggested this even without prior knowledge. The furnishings were contemporary chain-store, the upholstery thin and somewhat scuffed, the lamps barely adequate for a room that had but two windows.

Nancy Moore's first open-eyed glance when she saw him standing there became instantly one of friendly surprise. Her blond hair was still pulled back and braided behind but no longer quite so neat; there was less eye shadow in evidence. The bare feet and the jersey-and-slack outfit gave her a casual, relaxed appearance. Her perfume, too, was less pronounced.

"Come in, Mr. Fenner. We're playing a little gin and I'm getting clobbered. You want to make it three-handed?"

Fenner grinned back at her and gave a small wave to Kathy Kennedy who was sitting at a rickety-looking card table, her quick smile complimentary and the Irish-blue eyes bright with interest. He declined the invitation with some amusement but by the time he sat down his lean face was sober and his green eyes grave as they flicked from one girl to the other.

"How're you making out?"

"Just fine," Nancy said. He saw then that she had a can of beer on a small low table next to her chair while Kathy had what looked like a soft drink. Nancy gestured with the can. "Would you like one?"

Fenner said no thanks and watched her take a swallow right from the can. He asked if they were keeping reasonably busy. What, for instance, did they do last night?

"Went to a movie," Kathy said.

"What time did you leave here, Kathy? I mean afterward?"

An exchange of glances and Nancy said: "Maybe eleven-thirty or so. Why?"

"Just wondering," he said casually. "What I came for was to tell Kathy she can wrap up this assignment, and to tell you you no longer need a protective companion. Someone shot Mark Haskell three times in his apartment early this morning."

The simple announcement brought a sudden hush to the room. It continued for some time. Kathy simply looked at him, the eyes wide open and lips parted. Nancy's narrow, pointed face was almost expressionless now, the blue eyes bleak and suspicious. Aware of the silence, she broke it, her voice flat.

"You don't know me well enough to try a put-on."

"No put-on," Fenner said. "Someone shot him when he opened the door to his apartment. He could have had a woman with him. The police aren't sure if he did, or what she might know. The point is that I had to tell them I was hired originally by Esterbrook & Warren. They've probably talked to George

Tyler by now and he has no reason not to tell them of Haskell's threats and harassment, and what I was doing to protect both you and Ben Clayton. So they'll be around sometime to confirm things with you. Have you still got that gun?"

She nodded, mouth tightening with some disapproval. "Do you want to see it? Why don't you just come out and say you're wondering if I used it?"

He waved the implication aside. "If you did you could be in trouble."

She rose stiffly, left the room, and came back with the little automatic. He saw then that it was a Berretta, a .22 by the looks of it; full clip, no noticeable odor.

"They'll be checking on your boyfriend," he said, returning the gun, "if they haven't already. He could have some explaining to do too. You may want to phone him."

He glanced at Kathy Kennedy. "Do you want to call your boss or shall I?"

"You can explain things better. I'll get my things."

"I think a full eight hours today would be fair." He looked at Nancy. "Is that all right with you? . . . And yesterday," he added to Kathy when there was no reply, "you were on from one until eleven-thirty—call it midnight, eleven hours."

He looked again at Nancy. "You got off cheap. If someone hadn't done you a favor this could have gone on until Monday. But I guess you're not really interested, are you?"

The dry, sardonic tone finally got to her. She took a large breath, breasts thrusting. When she let it out she was once again relaxed and the suspicion, animosity, resentment, whatever it was, vanished.

"Sorry," she said, her smile twisted, "I didn't mean to be difficult. I loved having Kathy with me and I appreciate your getting someone so nice. In a way I'm almost sorry she has to leave. Does she have to? I mean, couldn't she stay, like she did last night?"

The request surprised Fenner and he showed it. "Well sure.

I thought you might want to have dinner with the boyfriend."

"Not tonight," she said firmly. "If the police come around with their questions I'd rather have Kathy with me."

Fenner glanced at Kathy, saw her small nod of agreement and said: "Okay then, whatever you decide is fine with me."

14

Jack Fenner did not stay long at Marion Haskell's borrowed apartment. She greeted him cheerfully, the hazel eyes friendly after the first moment of surprise, and it was difficult for him to remember that she knew nothing of what had happened to her husband. For this seemed obvious from her gracious manner as she waved him to a chair and perched on the edge of the sofa, knees together, feet flat on the floor, clasped hands resting on her thighs. He heard her ask if Ben Clayton was all right, and he nodded, wondering how to start and then saying the first thing that came to mind.

"I take it the police haven't been here yet."

"Police?" She peered at him as if he were across the room. "Good heavens no! Why on earth should they? Aren't you and Ben the only ones who know where I am?"

"I'm afraid it won't be like that long. You see, someone shot your husband last night at his apartment. Someone who was standing in the hall when he opened the door. Probably died instantly."

For a long moment then the face went pale and slack, her eyes enormous with shock and disbelief. When the words finally came they were hushed and choked with sudden fear.

"Oh, my God! Not Ben?"

"I said your husband, Mrs. Haskell. Mark."

"Mark? But—what—I mean how?"

Fenner cut her off and kept talking, his phrases blunt, direct, and clipped because he wanted her to understand and this seemed the best way. This took no more than three minutes and there was no interruption. Gradually the color returned to her cheeks. She had leaned back in an attitude of weariness and resignation, but by the time he had finished much of her composure had returned.

"I see," she said finally. "And now I guess Ben and I and the others don't have to worry any more, do we? Do the police know who did it, or why?"

"Not yet. They may have some thoughts on why. I talked to Mr. Clayton. He didn't know Haskell had been killed either. I reminded him that you had to be told because the police always suspect a wife in a murder where there is another woman involved. He said he'd rather I came to tell you because he expected to be a bit busy with the police this afternoon."

"Ben? The police. But why should they—"

"Because they're going to find out what's behind all this. Those threats your husband made will come out. Clayton is obviously involved in some way. Fortunately he spent the night at my place," he added and explained the circumstances.

There was distance in her gaze by the time he had finished, and a small smile came, apparently at some secret thing.

"Poor Ben," she said softly. "He must have been frightfully upset or desperate or something. He almost never got that way. It was nice of you to see that he stayed with you. He just might have got himself into some kind of trouble."

Fenner said Clayton was a little wild but he made no mention of the threats or the loaded gun the man had carried. However this thought prompted a question.

"Do you have a handgun, Mrs. Haskell?"

"A handgun?" She made it sound preposterous. "Like a pistol? Certainly not."

"I thought Mr. Clayton might have given you one for protection."

"He most certainly did not," she said indignantly. As an afterthought she added: "Supposing he had given me one?"

"Then it might be a good idea to get rid of it before the police get here." He leaned forward, accenting his words. "All this may seem somewhat absurd and academic to you but don't kid yourself. The police could give you a hard time and they have a right to their suspicions. Because this is not just a company stock fight; it's the personal sort of thing that often leads to murder or violence.

"You were married to Ben Clayton and Haskell wanted you. He practically paid Harry Bascomb to set up that strip-poker game. And Haskell lied and needled and conned you into believing Clayton had always been promiscuous or something like that—"

"It was just my silly outraged female pride," she said, interrupting. "I made the mistake of listening to a man who was a liar and a cheat and a bully and—"

Fenner cut her off abruptly. "But don't forget, you were planning to divorce Haskell and he must have known it. You went to the trouble of having a private investigator get the necessary evidence—and the police will find that out too. And recently Haskell mistreated you and kept you a prisoner in your own home and Clayton got you out and put you here where Haskell couldn't reach you. Believe me, Mrs. Haskell, every bit of this is going to come out eventually."

"What you're saying"—she was making an effort to be precise —"is that I am under suspicion for murder."

"At least temporarily."

"Ben too?"

"Ben especially if it weren't for his alibi."

"But there must be someone else. I know I didn't kill my husband and I'm just as positive that Ben didn't either."

"You're right there," Fenner said and spoke some of Monty

Saxton, his mistress, and his current problems. "Your husband owed Saxton an awful lot of money. With the interest Saxton charges, a settlement might be impossible if it weren't for money he would have realized when the company takeover was completed. Saxton was there last night but the police can't put him on the scene at the right time. Which doesn't mean they won't. They'll be combing the neighborhood for possible witnesses while they try to break down his alibi."

He stood up and said he had to run. "You might try Mr. Clayton at his office. He can tell you more how things stand with him. You won't have to stay here any longer, though it may be more convenient. What I would do is get in touch with Esterbrook & Warren, or whoever handles your affairs, and let some attorney surrender you for questioning. You can tell Mr. Clayton what I said and see what he thinks."

She rose then as he turned toward the door, her face thoughtful and the hazel eyes troubled. The cadence of her voice was unmistakably appreciative when she thanked him for coming.

The address Fenner had for Sandra Joslin was, he knew, a sizable but by no means exclusive apartment house named the Ashton Arms. Because she had not been in the city long enough to have a listed telephone he had an idea calls reached her through a switchboard. He had stopped on his way there to phone and ask for the Joslin apartment, pleased when a woman answered. Wanting only to know if she was in he had said: "Is this the Mitchell residence? . . . Oh, sorry. I must have the wrong number."

No one stopped him on his way to one of the two automatic elevators and he went along the fourth floor hall until he came to four-H. He felt his tie and straightened his jacket after he had pushed the recessed button. The instant he heard the knob turn he put on what he hoped was one of his most engaging smiles.

The girl who swung the door wide with no apparent thought of caution fulfilled satisfactorily the complimentary descriptions he had been given by others. Even in sandals she stood a good five-feet-seven or better, with broad shoulders and bright blond hair that curled upward at the ends. The lounging suit, if that was the proper term, was the snug kind that did much for the solid-looking hips and thighs. There was a certain commonness about the face with its broad jaw and cheekbones, some flatness in profile perhaps because of the nose, and the wide painted mouth seemed always to be revealing the white even teeth, suggesting that this mannerism, artificial though it was, had been modeled on Raquel Welch or one of her many imitators.

The greenish eyes, artfully shadowed and slightly upward-slanting at the corners, looked right at him in that first second or two, their expression curious, observant, and attentive.

Her drawled, yes, had a deep-south inflection and she stood holding the edge of the door while Fenner introduced himself and showed his identification.

"Oh?" She examined his face again, still interested. "Are you sure you have the right apartment?"

"If you're Miss Joslin, yes," said Fenner, knowing instantly that this was the voice on the Haskell tapes.

"And you'd like to come in?"

"If it's all right." Fenner kept his smile constant and deliberately approving. "For a few minutes."

The broad shoulders shrugged expressively beneath the cream-colored pullover, the full breasts moving a bra thin enough to be pleasantly revealing.

"All right," she said and stood back. "For a little while, depending what you want and how nice you are. I mean, we could at least have a drink I guess."

She turned then and led the way into the living room, trailing the odor of perfume that, unlike Nancy Moore's, was stronger, headier, and too generously applied. Here she picked up a half-filled glass from a nearby table and waved to the far corner where a railed wooden tray rested on a collapsible stand. The room, he noticed then, was larger than Nancy Moore's rented one, and though it had somehow a furnished look, it was far more comfortable, with deeply cushioned chairs, a pillowed divan along one wall, and a pale-green carpet in good condition.

She came up behind him as he fixed his Bourbon and water. Handing him her now empty glass, she said: "Scotch and soda," and then left him to fix her drink.

When he turned with the two glasses she was at ease on the divan, arms outstretched along the back to make more noticeable her abundant bustline, and indicated with a head signal that he was to place her glass on the coffee table. Fenner took the nearest chair and her perfume enveloped him like some unseen smog.

"Now Mr. Investigator, how did you know my name was Joslin? I mean, like, how did you find me, and why bother?"

Fenner took his time while he made a mental assessment of what made this girl tick. There was somehow a blatant sexuality, like the scent she wore, that was impossible to ignore; it was also likely that she had been aware of it since her mid-teens and was both pleased and proud that she had been so handsomely endowed. There was a certain earthiness here, part worldly and part naïve, and he guessed that in addition to her own selfish pleasures she was equally concerned about economic and material things. In short a dame he would love to spend a no-phone-calls, do-not-disturb weekend with and still be grateful that he was not married to her.

He had purposely brought a copy of the *Courier's* evening edition. He had known there would have been time to cover the Haskell story, though not in depth, and the essentials were there on page three. Now opening and folding the copy, with the story and two-column head face up, he placed it on the low table.

"Have you seen the afternoon paper?"

"No."

"I thought you might be interested in this," he said and touched the story with his fingernail.

She sat up then, slowly at first and perhaps more from idle

curiosity than anything else. The greenish eyes, narrowed slightly now, continued to inspect him until she had leaned forward. Then the reaction came and she hunched still farther forward, arms crossed and elbows tucked tight into her middle. He could see the penciled brows snap high, the movement of the scanning eyes, the slow seep of color from her cheeks. She was not a fast reader and it took rather long, but when she looked up the eyes were scared, bewildered, and full of shock.

When she finally spoke she made a show of defiance, but it was not convincing because of some unsteadiness in the vocal cords she could not control. He understood then that she could not communicate verbally without resorting to the growing bastard usage of three overworked and all too common expressions.

In order they were: like—I mean—you know?

"So what about it?" she demanded. "A guy gets himself killed last night. Am I supposed to care? I mean, why should you think so?"

"You don't know Mark Haskell?"

"Well, sure, like, you know, I've seen him around. He stopped in a while ago for a drink with m—my boyfriend."

"The one that's paying the rent?"

She pulled herself erect on the cushion and glared at him, mouth working. "All right. Just what the hell do you want? If you've got something to say, say it; if not buzz off."

"If you say so." Fenner gestured with the glass. "But I thought maybe you'd want to rehearse your story before you told it to the police."

"Police? Are you nuts? What story?"

"About where you were last night and what time you left Mark Haskell's apartment . . . Oh, they won't have any trouble there," Fenner added, exaggerating some. "You were seen by two of my men coming in around nine-thirty. The description was perfect. They didn't see you leave, not before one-thirty anyway. Before the cops finish they'll know when you left. Not that it matters. You were there, and in bed—they have some blond hairs—and you'd finished your love-making and someone pounded on the door . . . Did you know Haskell had bugged that bed?"

"Bugged?" She stared at him, aghast, the fear and consternation showing. "You mean, like with a microphone and all that. For God's sake why? I mean, was he that kind of kook?"

Fenner told her about the frame under the bed to hold the recorder, explained the pressure switch.

"Why?" he said. "Because he was in hock to Saxton and he wanted something he could use to force a settlement. Like your pillow talk, and bits about Saxton's wife Sylvia, and his business, and how he brought you up from New Orleans."

"You're making it up," she said, her voice now merely a whisper.

"I heard one of the tapes. The police have both of them. They obviously weren't made last night but sometime earlier. My guess is Haskell wasn't using one last night because he'd already had enough."

He waved the glass to indicate the room. "This is a very nice place. Rent paid in cash the first of the month. I understand you've got plenty of clothes, including a mink coat. A fat bank balance, all provided—unless you were turning a trick on the side—by Saxton. Just what was it Haskell had to offer?"

She leaned forward, swallowed half her drink, and put the glass down hard.

"Not what you think. I guess I'm just stupid. Mark didn't pay me a dime. He gave me a few presents. And I really did meet him here, a couple of months ago. Monty introduced him. Afterwards he, you know, phoned me, asked me to meet him for a drink. And goddamnit I *was* bored. Sitting around, I mean, like knowing Monty would probably be here only one night a week, having to go out alone all the time—

"I liked Mark. He was nice to me, and thoughtful, and Monty was out all night Tuesdays anyway. He wasn't like some of the others, I mean Mark. He was good. I liked it. Not one of those guys that use you and reach for their pants. He liked to talk afterward and—"

She stopped again, as though she had begun to make the proper association and conclusion. She took the rest of her drink and sank back on the cushions, her voice small and still bewildered.

"That's all he wanted, hunh? The talk. Wanting me to rat on Monty, the sonofabitch. I thought—well, that kind of talk, afterward I mean, is the friendliest kind . . . I guess you think I'm just another call girl," she added softly. "Well, maybe, but not really. I mean, I wasn't available to just anyone. I had, you know, two or three friends in New Orleans, that's all. And Monty was there for some meeting and we went out and he said how about coming north with him, that he'd set me up and treat me right, and give me a nice allowance, and I could leave any time."

Fenner nodded. He'd known girls like Sandra Joslin before, not many but enough to understand. Not hookers or full-time call girls with no other known profession. Not pickups, or those who regardless of sponsorship made dates over the phone; not clients of some madam either. All had jobs of one sort or another —secretaries, receptionists, models. Careful and particular. Never having more than two or three regular friends, almost always married men who felt they needed, and could afford, an afternoon or evening of relaxed sex that was mutually enjoyable and perhaps even beneficial . . .

"I'm sorry."

"I said I'd never been up this way before and I thought, you know, like I could fatten my bank account without doing much for it—"

"And you did, didn't you? You should be in pretty good shape."

"Well, so what?"

"Saxton went there last night."

"Went where?"

"To Haskell's. You must have heard him banging on the door."

Fenner noticed the change instantly and rebuked himself for hurrying things. The distance that had been in her gaze changed to wariness and now a small and twisted smile came.

"How could I hear any banging? I wasn't there."

"You didn't hear the three shots either then," Fenner said dryly.

"Certainly not. Like I say, how could I? Your people may have seen Haskell come in with some blond earlier. Does that make it me? Who says so? If the cops thought—"

Fenner cut in again, knowing what she was about to say. "I had a little edge because Haskell's wife had a man checking him out a while back. That's how I got your name and address. Since you're clean there's no reason why I shouldn't—"

He got that far when the room buzzer sounded twice. They rose together, looking at each other, Fenner's gaze curious and the girl's quickly concerned. When he asked if she wanted him to answer it she said, her voice strangely listless now:

"All right."

Fenner opened the door, half expecting Bacon or one of his men; then he was staring at Monty Saxton who stared back, a neat and dapper figure in a dark-gray topcoat and black hat. Neither spoke in the first moment of recognition; then Saxton's quick dark eyes slid beyond and found the girl.

Ignoring Fenner now, he brushed past and addressed her, his voice tight, clipped, and mean.

"What the hell is he doing here? What did you let him in for? Goddamnit! Didn't you know he was a private cop? Feeding him drinks even, entertaining him while you spill your guts."

"I didn't spill anything," she said hotly. "Honest, Monty. Sure I knew who he was; he showed me his identification. But he seemed nice enough, and polite and—damn it all I was lonely. I've been telling you—"

"Shut up!"

"All right, all right," she said forlornly and collapsed on the divan, hands covering her face and the blond head bowed. "I guess I'm on my way back to New Orleans anyway," she said through her fingers.

Saxton spun back to glare at Fenner, the meanness still there. "You," he said. "Blow! And don't come back."

15

Jack Fenner had his solitary dinner in a small Italian place where they served the best spaghetti in town. Its clientele was almost exclusively regulars, the operation a family one, and he had been stopping in every week or ten days for some time, attracted not only by the food but by the certain knowledge that no one he knew would be likely to interrupt his privacy.

Hardly aware of his surroundings after the first familiar greeting and the proprietor's personal attention, he ordered a very dry martini, spaghetti with mushroom sauce, a green salad, and a small bottle of Chianti. By the time the martini had done its work he was hungry, and he enjoyed the meal, a remoteness in his gaze and a brooding but not forbidding look on his angular face as he sorted his thoughts.

He felt immeasurably better when he finished and considered momentarily having a brandy with his coffee. Then, remembering he still had some good Martell's at home and wanting more time to enjoy it, he paid his check with its customary tip, was ushered elegantly to the door, and left with the cheery good wishes of the proprietor and his wife.

He had been home no more than ten minutes when the trouble hit, and looking back on it he knew they must have been parked down the street awaiting his arrival. They had no trouble gaining entrance downstairs because, while this was a brownstone similar to the one where Mark Haskell stayed, its remodeling had been minimum and the heavy downstairs door seldom latched properly, no great disadvantage since outwardly the building would offer slight promise to a burglar.

He had his jacket off and had taken his first, savoring mouthful of the brandy before he measured more into a highball glass, adding soda and ice. He had reached the center of the living room when the knock came and he took a good swallow before he put the glass aside and went to the door, more curious than annoyed.

They came in with confidence, deliberate and purposeful, and he knew instantly what they had in mind. As he stepped back, measuring the two, his cop's instinct went to work and he understood that his best chance was to move first and without hesitation.

Experience over the years also enabled him to recognize the types: the slim neat youth in the dark business suit, blue shirt, and yellow tie, the blank thin face and the almost colorless eyes; the big man, older, beefy but not all fat, sloppy, bent-nosed, a good two hundred and forty pounds.

The big man said: "Hello Fenner," and closed the door behind him. And Fenner waited, poised, hands at side, measuring his chances. He could see the slight bulge made by the thin man's shoulder holster but there was no movement yet. But the big man was inching up, a fixed humorless grin working on the puffy face that might have been anticipation. And Fenner knew he had seen him around. He almost had a name—Monty, no. Marty, that was it.

Ignoring the gun now and hoping surprise would help him there, he shifted his weight so he stood at an angle, sensing somehow that one normal punch, no matter how good, would not be enough, that if the big man could bring his weight to bear it would be all over. So when the other stuck his chin out slightly, exposing the neck, Fenner chopped viciously at the

Adam's apple, his palm and fingers rigid, the blow slashing horizontally with the hard edge of the hand.

He knew the vulnerability of that spot in the anatomy and the blow was perfectly executed and Marty went back a step, not falling but sinking to one knee, gagging, choking, both hands clasped to his neck.

Then Fenner spun in a continuation of the same expert move, seeing the gun coming out as surprise transfixed the thin man, clearing the holster but not quite pointing. This time he struck, not at the unprotected jaw but sharply at the wrist. He caught it just at the base of the thumb and the short-barrel revolver flew sideways, and he did not watch but stepped close and hooked with his left.

This time the man went down. He wasn't hurt but he was on his rump, the surprise and bewilderment there for a second before he understood what had happened. By the time he had rolled to his feet Fenner had recovered the gun and stepped back, waiting and seeing the hate and venom building in the colorless eyes.

Marty was still on one knee, doubled over like a man with his wind knocked out. The continuing throaty, gasping, hawking sounds said he was having trouble getting his breath, and when he finally got his head up his mouth was bloodstained from some internal hemorrhaging. Fenner understood this because he had seen it before: but Marty didn't. When he wiped his lips with the back of his hand and found it red, he stared in disbelief, too fascinated by his discovery to present any immediate problem.

Fenner began to breathe again. Somewhere at the back of his throat there was a dryness and he swallowed to get rid of it. Now he watched the thin youth shake himself and shrug his jacket into place. The narrowed gaze was fixed on Fenner's face, the mouth a gash. Fenner had seen such eyes before on killers, the odd icy brightness that somehow reflected neither pity, compassion, nor conscience.

Moving forward no more than a foot, ignoring the gun, the

youth stuck his face out a little more and, the viciousness still there, said: "You're a dead man Fenner!"

Fenner understood it later but right then there was only the savage, unaccountable instinct to destroy that leering face and he reacted brutally.

It was not a pretty punch but it was powerful and devastating, an overhand right that landed flush in the middle of that face, jarring his forearm and shoulder and blotting out the features as the other went backward and fell heavily and flat on his back.

Still conscious but unable for the moment to rouse himself he lay there and Fenner saw that Marty, though on his feet now, still had one hand on his neck, and the stupid expression, the obvious docility, told him that Marty was through for the night. Even so he tried to speak, the voice no more than a croak.

"You bastard. You slugged me when I wasn't looking."

"You were looking all right, Marty. You just got overconfident. What were you supposed to do, break an arm or two?"

"Nah! Just work you over."

"Then why the punk with the piece?"

"It wasn't my idea."

"I know whose idea it was," Fenner said thinly, "and we'll get to that in a minute."

He saw then that the thin man was on his knees and getting up, a bit wobbly but determined. His nose was bleeding and slightly aslant. One lip was split and the mouth was bloody too. But the eyes were the same. Vicious, hateful, and determined, they stayed fixed as he came close again and said in the same cold threatening tones:

"I'm going to kill you, Fenner. You can believe it."

The hot resentment that had flared before and was fed too often by such men who had been arrested and freed came back and he swung again. The same savage blow, the desire to punish, to retaliate, the certainty that the other would have killed him without mercy.

This time the youth fell backward, but limply, unjointed,

helpless. For a second Fenner surveyed him, aware that he was shaking, the knees unsteady with some weakness flowing through his body as reaction set in. His throat was dry again and he had to swallow once more, wondering what had happened to his saliva glands. He looked down at the gun in his left hand and noticed the palm was damp with sweat as he slipped it into his hip pocket. He considered the raw redness of the first three knuckles on his right hand, sucked them absently, and spoke to Marty.

"Sit down, Marty, and stay put. I'll be right back."

Either Marty was used to obeying commands when uttered in threatening tones or he was still a bit unsteady from some physical reaction; in any event he was sitting quite still except for the one hand that was gently massaging his neck when Fenner returned with a soaking facecloth.

The thin youth had begun to move and with Fenner's help managed a sitting position, his back against the wall. The pale eyes apparently had little capacity for any normal emotion and he had difficulty focusing them. The sharp-featured face was a mess. The thin nose, oozing blood, had been obviously broken at least once, the lips were gashed and swollen and the front teeth did not look right. The once-yellow tie was mostly crimson now and the blood was still dripping slowly onto the blue shirt when Fenner put the wet cloth over the bottom of the face and told him to hold it.

Then, backing a step and no longer worried about Marty, he felt a brief thrust of shame, guilt, and embarrassment that he could respond so savagely, so impulsively, to those taunting threats that had been uttered in that cold and menacing voice. For a few seconds he could not quite understand how he could have let himself go like that; then the answer came to him and he accepted it.

True, he had no alternative but to attack quickly and in any way he could if only to save his own skin. Once he'd put the youth down and had possession of the gun the thing was done and he had won. But the leering, vicious, barefaced threat, the long-remembered experiences with others little different from this hoodlum still rankled. In uniform, and later in plainclothes, he had been powerless to retaliate to such threats. To do so meant almost certain release of the prisoner for one reason or another, and almost surely some disciplinary measures by his superiors.

The arrogance of the knowledgeable offender no matter how brutal or heinous the crime seemed only to aggravate the frustration which built insidiously each time they walked out free men, or on bond, to repeat the same offense. A slap or two, not in the mouth where it might show, a jab in ribs or belly, a twisted arm—that was the extent of any physical contact, and it came to Fenner now that all he had done was to give vent finally to a reaction heretofore prohibited and too long suppressed. When he was ready for Marty he felt neither shame nor satisfaction, other than that which comes to an artisan for a job well done.

"Now, Marty. Let's talk, hunh?"

He pulled a straight-backed chair up to face the sullen and resentful Marty, reversing it as he sat down and letting the gun dangle from one hand as he leaned on crossed forearms.

"You want to walk out of here," he said in even tones, "you're going to make a little phone call. I'm not going to waste time asking who sent you because I think I know. So move over there by that telephone table."

Marty thought it over, heavy face working and the little eyes puzzled and uncertain. Fenner prodded him verbally.

"You and the punk brought the gun so if I put one in your kneecap I'd only be protecting my home, right?"

Marty sort of leaned forward and came to his feet. "Who do I call?"

"The boss. You've muscled for Monty Saxton from time to time and I don't know who else would be interested in leaning on me right now."

"I don't know where he is."

"You know some numbers, Marty. He's probably waiting to hear from you so get with it. You get him or I bring in the law right now."

Some flicker of hope seemed to brighten the big man's eyes. "You mean maybe you won't call the law if I get a hold of Monty? What do I say to him?"

"What do you usually call him? I mean to his face?"

"Mr. Saxton. Or sometimes boss."

"Okay. Now here's what you tell him, and get it right the first time. You tell him you're at Jack Fenner's and something came up and it's important that he come right away and you'll be waiting for him. Don't give him a chance to argue; hang up."

"Then what?"

"Then we wait, Marty, we wait." . . .

It took Saxton twelve minutes to make it and when Fenner went over to get the door he had the gun in his right hand. Saxton seemed to see it first judging from the movement of his shadowed dark eyes. While he was doing so Fenner sized up the man behind the gambler, recognizing him as the young blond husky he had seen in Saxton's office.

They stood like that for perhaps five seconds, a silent tableau as Saxton's gaze moved beyond to survey the room and Marty and the thin man who, sitting in a chair now, still had the wet cloth to the bottom half of his face.

"I should have had Marty tell you to come alone," Fenner said finally.

"So?"

"So tell your boy to go back and sit in the car and we'll talk, or the two of you back off and I'll handle this some other way."

Saxton studied him a moment as if he were some slide specimen, spoke over his shoulder. "You heard him, Al. Go back and wait."

Fenner moved back. Saxton stepped inside and closed the

door. The look he gave Marty was both disgusted and contemptuous.

"So you couldn't handle him, huh, you slob? I told you he might be tough."

"You should've told us he was sneaky," Marty mumbled defensively and drew a finger across his throat. "He damn near broke my neck."

"And what was little Joey doing then?" said Saxton in the same tone as he considered the thin youth.

"He wasn't fast enough."

"What happened to his face? . . . Let's see, Joey."

The youth lowered the cloth and Saxton shook his head, then considered Fenner. "How come you messed him up like that?"

"After I'd dumped him and had the gun he stuck his nose in my face and said I was a dead man so I slugged him." He displayed his reddened knuckles. "So then he comes up again and says he's going to kill me, that it's a promise. I figured I'd better get my licks in while I could."

Saxton nodded, still thoughtful. He unbuttoned his coat and tipped the brim of his hat back an inch.

"What have you got in mind?"

"They can walk out of here on two conditions. One, this punk"—he nodded at Joey—"leaves town tonight on the first plane. He's imported, isn't he? From where?"

"Detroit. He's only been here two days."

"Have Marty phone the airport and see what's leaving Logan tonight westbound and get a seat."

A nod was sufficient to get Marty moving and Saxton said: "Fair enough. What's number two?"

"When we're alone we have a talk."

"That's all?"

"That's all."

They stood that way, listening to Marty on the telephone until the big man covered the mouthpiece.

"There's a seat on one at ten-fifty."

"Tell them to hold it in your name. You'll pick it up at the terminal."

Marty did as directed and when he hung up he said: "What about his face?"

"Yeah." It was the first word Joey had uttered and the loosened teeth and mashed mouth made the rest of it sound distorted. "And who pays for the dentist?"

"Send me a bill, you stupid jerk," Saxton snarled. Then to Marty: "You know where to take him to get him patched up good enough to travel, and see if you can get this right. You'll stay with him, understand? Until he's on the plane and you see it take off. Now get out." He took a fold of bills from his pocket and peeled off two fifties.

Marty took them and shuffled toward the door. Joey stood up, his broken face still damp with blood. When Fenner told him to leave the facecloth he looked at it with distaste, held one corner between thumb and finger as though it was contaminated; then dropped it insolently on the carpet. He followed Marty out without a word, his pale eyes avoiding Saxton.

"You got a drink?" Saxton said when the door closed.

Fenner, remembering his brandy and soda, finished it off and said: "In the kitchen."

He fixed a fresh one and waited until Saxton poured a large slug of Scotch over ice and took a swallow. All this was done in silence and when Saxton gave Fenner an upward, appraising glance Fenner said:

"Let's go in and sit down."

"In a minute." Saxton took another swallow and poured more Scotch.

In the living room Fenner sat down on the davenport and told Saxton to sit in the club chair diagonally in front of it. The suggestion had a definite purpose but Saxton could not know this, or that there was a tape recorder and microphone in one of the two pieces of furniture that served as end tables.

The tops and legs were of genuine antique construction and Fenner had a cabinetmaker construct two cupboards underneath that had louvres in the front. One was simply used as a catchall; the other held the recorder activated by a hidden switch underneath the overhang of the top. Now, as Fenner put his drink on this table, he surreptitiously flicked the switch.

"All right, Monty, let's get down to it, just you and me. Why did you send those two punks to lean on me?"

"Because sometimes, not often, but sometimes, I am a very stupid guy. Especially when I'm mad."

"How far were they supposed to go?"

"Far enough so you'd remember it for a while."

"Why the gun punk?"

"In case Marty couldn't handle you." Saxton sipped some Scotch, put the glass aside and took out a leather cigar case. He offered one, was refused, and carefully lit his own with a gold lighter. "What set me off," he said when he had settled back comfortably, "was finding you there with Sandra. I knew damn well you'd probably been questioning her, and she'd been drinking—"

He broke off with an angry impatient oath and said: "Then a couple of hours ago she phoned and said the police had been there questioning her. I thought you'd tipped them off. She'd said something about a private dick tailing Haskell a while back and learning she'd been shacking up with him at his place on my poker nights. I thought I'd teach you a lesson."

"That wasn't me. That happened some time ago because Mrs. Haskell put a man on him to get divorce evidence. I got Sandra's name and address from his report."

"So I jumped to conclusions. When a guy pushes me too hard I like to push back. I was too burned to think it out." Saxton shrugged and dismissed the subject. "Like I said, with you I made a mistake. What do you want to do about it, press charges? Go to it if you think it will do you any good."

"I'd rather talk about those tapes. And don't ask me what

tapes because Bacon already has two and I heard part of one. You don't think Haskell set up that rig for his own amusement, do you?"

"I know why he set them up."

"So do I, I think. But how do *you* know?"

"Because I got one in the mail, sent anonymously, yesterday morning."

"Let me guess a little, okay? How much were you into Haskell, originally and presently?"

"Around sixty grand, what he owed me and the IOUs I bought up at eighty cents on the dollar." A thin grin twitched one corner of his mouth as he hesitated. "Now better than a hundred."

"The interest you charge mounts up fast."

The grin became more noticeable. "We offer a very necessary service to businessmen who, for one reason or another, can't get an additional loan from their bank. Sometimes it can tide them over and—"

"Sometimes you arrange a partnership," Fenner finished dryly. "How many shares of Haskell & Company did Mark have to put up to stay healthy?"

"A few."

"So he got to your girl. With his outward charm and his experience with women I don't imagine it was too hard. He must have known she was a high-priced call girl who might be willing to share an evening now and then."

"With Sandra he'd have no trouble at all if she could be sure I didn't catch her at it."

"And with maybe too much of your holdings in your wife's name, plus your current trouble with Internal Revenue, you'd be over a barrel all ways if Haskell went to the wife with proof of your continued cheating. The other tape for the IOUs, Monty. Is that how it was?"

Saxton chewed on his cigar and finished his drink. When he stayed silent Fenner said: "And no assurance that even if you agreed he might not still have copies of those tapes for later use.

That's why you cut out of your poker game early and went to his place last night, right?"

"The bastard wouldn't let me in."

"So you went back a couple or three hours later with a gun, somehow talked him into opening the door, and used it."

The dark eyes, no longer shadowed by the hat brim, were shrewd and cunning now, the voice sardonic.

"Even if I did—and with your word against mine meaning nothing—I wouldn't admit it. If the cops think so let 'em prove it."

"Your girl could have still been there. If you said anything at all she could have recognized your voice, ever think of that?"

Saxton's mustache moved, the line of his mouth contemptuous. "The only one who can put me at Haskell's place at all is that ex-cop grifter Kinlaw, and when he thinks it over he could change his mind about that . . . Thanks for the drink, Fenner. Sorry about the boys busting in on you, but then you came out all right, didn't you?"

"Just keep your friend Joey out of town."

"Don't worry. After the way he handled himself tonight I wouldn't let him sweep out my office. If I need help in the future I'll get me another boy." He stood up, a frown beginning to show. "One more thing. How about letting me have the punk's gun?"

Fenner slipped it from his hip pocket, weighed it in his palm. When he glanced up the green eyes were veiled and watchful.

"I don't think so, Monty. I may want to give it to Bacon before we're finished. You know, as a gesture of my good will."

"Sure," Saxton said, resentment showing.

"Or I might just turn it over to a friend of mine in ballistics to check and see if the slugs match anything in the files."

Saxton straightened his hat. He said: "Suit yourself," and started for the door. Fenner watched it close. To keep himself from thinking too much he picked up the red-stained facecloth and took it into the bathroom, discarding it in the hamper.

When he returned he went around emptying ashtrays and collecting glasses.

The room seemed to reek of whisky and tobacco smoke and he shook his head distastefully as he turned out the lights and headed for the cleaner air of his bedroom. Drinking last night with Clayton and tonight with Saxton, no wonder the place stank.

16

With the bedside telephone off the hook, Jack Fenner slept well and was pleased that he felt alert and rested as he came awake. The sun was out again and the bedside clock said nine o'clock when he put the telephone back in its cradle. He had just reached the bathroom door when its shrill ring startled him.

Back on the edge of the bed and still naked he said: "Hello," and the clipped, impatient voice of Lieutenant Bacon came to him without preliminaries. "Who the hell have you been gassing with at this time in the morning?" Without waiting for a reply, he added: "I'm sending a car for you. Don't argue, just be out front in ten minutes or someone will come up and get you."

Fenner put the handset back gently, sighed in some annoyance and said, half aloud: "Now what, for God's sake?"

He went as he was to the kitchen and put the heat on high under the coffee water. By skipping his customary shower he was able to shave and get dressed and still have a taste of orange juice before he had his coffee. He was just finishing his first cup when he heard the horn blast twice outside and he took the final gulp, leaving the dirty cup and glass in the sink.

It was a marked patrol car with two uniformed men in front so he climbed into the back and got a cigarette going. They didn't say good morning, and neither did he. Because he knew better than to ask where they were going or why, he leaned back and enjoyed the smoke and the ride.

Five minutes later they turned down a street off Columbus Avenue in a district that, never fashionable, had deteriorated into a neighborhood of shabby three- and four-storied apartments that were by now fully integrated.

The ambulance out front of one of these gave him a clue. Two familiar-looking black four-door sedans told him the ambulance men had company. He had no idea who lived here and the driver was no help. He simply pointed to a doorway that stood open.

"Top floor. The lieutenant's expecting you."

"Thanks," said Fenner. "Thanks very much for the ride."

They grinned at the mild sarcasm and the rider even touched his cap. Fenner went up then through the noise of television programs, not all of them muted, and smells so complex they defied analysis and, to a sensitive nose, were basically unpleasant.

The door to the right of the landing was also open, a uniformed officer stationed to keep the neighbors in their place. The scene inside was instantly familiar but the victim remained unknown because the body was already being lifted on a stretcher. The blanket, strapped and covering the face and head, was proof enough that whoever was beneath would be D.O.A. at the hospital.

The examiner's man, the same one who had been at Haskell's apartment the previous morning, followed the stretcher out. This gave a little more space in the front room which was nicer and more comfortable than he had expected considering the neighborhood and the building itself.

The technical experts were already busy and two plainclothesmen he did not know glanced round and nodded absently. Opposite the outer door was a wider doorway and he moved that way when he saw Bacon's tall, straight-backed figure in its all-gray trademark. As he reached the doorway he saw that the smaller room, apparently originally a dining room, had been used as an office. There was a littered desk by the lone window, a couple of chairs, a stack of metal filing cabinets, and an old typewriter on a separate stand.

Only then did Fenner start to speculate, his thoughts moving speedily until he asked himself, who do I know that has his office, at least part-time, at home? When he glanced up and found Bacon studying him with those shrewd gray eyes, he took a chance.

"Jake Kinlaw?"

"Intuition maybe?"

"Based on knowing Jake only had desk space downtown and must have kept most of his things at home."

"Two slugs this time, same general chest area but not so close up. We think it could be the same gun."

He stepped aside, pointing, and Fenner then saw the chalk-marked outline behind the desk and the revolver with a five-inch barrel on top.

"The gun was there?" he asked. "Jake's?"

"On the floor beside the body. He must have fired once. The slug's in the other room, the wall at the end." He pointed again to a tiny scar in the faded wallpaper behind the desk. "That one went clean through him. The other is still in him, probably hit a bone . . . How high would you say that was?"

"Three feet, probably more."

"And the wounds were chest high. One through the heart or a big artery according to the doc's guess, the other four or five inches diagonally up, probably not fatal."

Fenner waited patiently, not quite sensing where such comments were leading. Bacon glanced at the scar, removed his hat, and finger-combed his thick gray hair which was getting shaggy at the nape. When he had replaced the hat he continued.

"So unless the killer was a midget Kinlaw wasn't standing up. Neither was he seated. My guess, he was coming out of his chair, sensing he was going to get it, but getting off a shot anyway, possibly wildly but more likely too late."

"What's the examiner say about time?"

"He made his usual guess but for once we don't need it. The shots were heard, but like most times the witnesses don't agree. It was the time for the TV cowboys and the shoot-outs, and the private dicks gunning down the villains—but before the eleven o'clock news. The guesses go from sometime after ten to a few minutes before eleven. Sit down somewhere," he said, and went into the front room to confer with Sergeant Gaynor.

Fenner took a nondescript wooden chair that looked as if it had been painted at least twice. He lit a cigarette, his narrowed gaze fixed on the irregular chalk outline on the carpet but not actually seeing it. He stayed that way, the cigarette burning down between his fingers by itself until Bacon returned, fanned out his coattails and perched a thigh and hip on one corner of the desk.

"We're about finished here but I'm expecting company. While we're waiting let's talk some."

Fenner cocked one brow, held it, nodded. "Okay. Who found him?"

"Lady next door. The television was on but so were a lot of others on the floor. Neighbors get used to neighbors listening to the late show, and the late late show; learn to sleep somehow in spite of this. But this old lady heard something on in here rather early this morning. She knew it was a TV but she couldn't figure what was on. You know the sound a set makes when you have it on and the station goes off the air? A lot of loud rasping nothing? Well that's what she heard so she gets dressed and finds the janitor, who comes up with a key. We got the call around eight."

Fenner nodded and Bacon looked right at him, head tipped slightly and a suggestion of a grin forming in the corners of his eyes.

"That attorney, George Tyler, was more cooperative than you were."

"I thought I was cooperative," Fenner said, playing along. "I told you who hired me and I didn't have to—" He put up his hand to forestall the interruption. "I mean, not just then."

"But not who hired you *after* the office conference."

"I thought it was better to come from him," Fenner said, not really meaning it.

"And when I assured Mr. Tyler," Bacon said as though he had not heard, "that I had no charges in mind therefore no arrests were imminent, he talked some. About the stock picture and Haskell's threats to your Mr. Clayton and the harassment to the girl—what's her name?"

"Nancy Moore."

"Not bad-looking, different somehow; a bit touchy, been around some. And her hired companion, Kathy Kennedy—who confirmed the assignment. And that actor boyfriend, Barry something or other."

He laughed abruptly, a sardonic sound. "The idiot had a gun, right there in his hotel room. You wouldn't believe what kind."

"No Saturday-night special?"

"The opposite."

"Could it be made to fit the Haskell job?"

"No way. A .32. Must've been fifty years old, an Iver Johnson tip-up model. Of course that doesn't mean he couldn't also have had a .38. A guy with one gun could have two. Some nuts I've run into have three or four. No alibi . . . Where was I? Oh, yeah. And we also called on Mr. Clayton and had a nice chat." He cocked his head again, half closing one eye. "Claims you as an alibi the night before last."

"He happens to be right."

"You could have told me yesterday morning."

"The client comes first so long as I'm not deliberately obstructing—"

"Balls!"

Bacon slid off the desk, turned around in some exasperation, and perched again with the other thigh. "He was there? Give me a schedule. From when to when?"

Fenner said he wasn't sure, which was the truth. "Got there maybe eleven or a bit later. Loaded."

"So he said. He could have been faking."

"Not his breath."

"And?"

"He wanted more. I gave it to him but I had to keep him company."

"Like how?"

"Like to drink along with him."

"Say why he came?"

"He was burned by Haskell's psycho methods and threats and tricks. I thought he might be in a drunken dangerous mood so I decided to try and keep him there."

"How do you mean dangerous?"

That one stopped Fenner. He wasn't sure how far to go or just how much the lieutenant had been told.

"What, or rather how much, did Clayton tell you?"

"I want to get it from you."

"Well, he had some crazy idea that the only way to keep Haskell from killing him—"

"He took those threats seriously?"

"Why not? He knew the guy."

"Go on."

"He said if he killed Haskell first he'd be sure Haskell didn't get him. I got the idea he was afraid he might do something foolish and came to me hoping I'd stop him."

Bacon nodded. When he had chewed on the information he said: "What time did you go to bed?"

"I'm not sure of that either."

"Guess."

"Midnight."

"Sleep well?"

"Very."

"So Haskell could have sneaked out during the night—"

"I don't buy it."

"I don't care what you buy. Can you swear that Clayton didn't leave while you were asleep? You did sleep some, didn't you?" he added pointedly.

"Yes, I slept," Fenner said, trying to be patient. "And no I can't swear to anything. But I do have some facts to substantiate—"

"Okay, let's hear them."

The request stopped Fenner momentarily. He wished now that he had told the lieutenant about Clayton's gun earlier. Why he had suspected it, how he had removed the shells—he still had them—when Clayton left the room. More important, his second inspection the following morning that told him the gun was clean, that even if Clayton *had* extra shells in his pants pocket he had not fired them. That was something Bacon could believe, but having withheld that information, he was reluctant to divulge it until he had a chance to consider carefully its importance. Now he substantiated his opinion as best he could.

"I say he had a load on when he came in—red-faced, bleary-eyed, a breath you could smell a block away. He had two more drinks with me, and believe me I slugged them; must have been close to four ounces in each. He was as good as out when I got a pillow and blanket for him."

"What time did you wake up?"

"Before dawn. Maybe five o'clock. When I remembered how he'd run off at the mouth I got up. Stood watching and listening to him breathe for a while before I went back to bed. When I finally got up to put on the coffee water he was in the same position."

Bacon moved his lips, his gaze remote. It was hard to tell what he was thinking and his next question came from left field.

"You know where we can find Mrs. Haskell?"

"You mean you haven't located her yet?" Fenner made his voice sound surprised, as though such an oversight was beyond belief. "What have *you* done to find her," he demanded, attacking to avoid the direct lie.

"What we always do. A six-state bulletin to pick up and hold. Back Bay and South Stations staked out; air terminals, bus stations. Her car is still at the Dedham place. We've been working on the hotels, motels, better rooming houses. Nothing yet. She's holed up somewhere is my guess. We're starting on the apartment hotels. It could take time but—"

"Clayton ought to know," Fenner said. "Why don't you ask him?"

"We have and will." Bacon glanced at his watch. "He should be here now."

"So," Fenner said, a crooked grin forming. "A little confrontation, hunh?"

Bacon's timing was excellent. Less than a minute later Sergeant Gaynor called from the front room to ask if Bacon wanted Mr. Clayton in there.

Ben Clayton came through the doorway with some hesitation, his light-brown eyes uncertain behind the glasses as they flicked from Bacon to Fenner and back again. Bacon slipped off the desk and said good morning.

"Why don't you take that chair there, Mr. Clayton. This shouldn't take too long."

Clayton, very neat and businesslike in his dark-blue worsted flannel suit, was looking at the chalked outline on the carpet as he moved the chair and eased down on it.

"I'm not quite sure why I'm here, Lieutenant. The officer who drove me over wasn't very informative."

"He wasn't supposed to be. Did you know a man named Jake Kinlaw?"

Clayton's mind was more alert than his attitude suggested. "Did? You mean something happened to him?" He listened to Bacon repeat the question and finally said: "I think he was one of the men Mr. Fenner employed to keep an eye on Mark Haskell."

"Right. He was on duty watching the Haskell place the night —or rather morning—that Haskell was shot. Last night someone came in here between ten and eleven and did the same thing to Kinlaw. Any idea why, Mr. Clayton?"

"Not the slightest. What makes you think I would?"

"We don't at the moment. What we're after is information. But we do have a theory. It goes like this." Bacon took his time, gray eyes steady and probing, his voice easy. "Kinlaw was watching that apartment until one-thirty, according to him. We know he saw one man who didn't belong there—not you, Mr. Clayton—enter and leave that building about eleven-thirty. Now Jake Kinlaw's record on the force was not very good. In fact he resigned rather than face an inquiry. So it occurs to us that either Kinlaw lied about the time he saw this man, or he saw someone else and decided to hold out that information for a while."

"Why would he do that?"

"Because, the way his mind worked, he just might have figured that by doing so he could set up a semipermanent pension plan of his own in return for silence or false evidence. It's been done before, sometimes successfully. The only hole in his plan was that he misjudged the man he intended, or tried, to blackmail . . . Now it would be pointless to attempt blackmailing someone who did not have the capacity to pay adequately for the risk he was taking, right? I suggest that you have that capacity, Mr. Clayton. Would you agree?"

"Yes, I suppose I could."

"So could our other man, who should be here shortly. Now would you mind telling me what you did last night from, say, seven o'clock on?"

"Not at all. I had an early dinner with Mrs. Haskell."

"Then you know where she is?"

"Well"—Clayton's glance slid to Fenner and he jerked it back —"yes."

"Where?"

Clayton mentioned the address. Bacon opened his mouth, closed it with some inner effort, exhaled noisily.

"Then you admit you lied to us yesterday?"

"I'm afraid I did."

"You'd have saved us, yes, and the agencies in some other

states, a hell of a lot of trouble if you'd volunteered that information, Mr. Clayton."

Clayton flushed at the rebuke and glanced away. "Sorry," he said stiffly. "I simply didn't want her bothered since she couldn't possibly know anything about Mark Haskell's murder."

"Maybe, maybe not. But I'm afraid we'll have to be the judge of just what she knows and doesn't know, and how it affects this case. Even if she can clear herself to our satisfaction she could have information that we can use. If I were you I'd be less concerned about Mrs. Haskell and more about yourself."

"Meaning I'm still under suspicion."

"You are indeed, Mr. Clayton. That's why you're here . . . Now what I'd like to know is why Mrs. Haskell moved out of the Dedham place."

"I took her out," Clayton said.

"Took in what sense?"

"Mark Haskell was holding her a virtual prisoner in the house. He had a female guard to keep her locked in her room."

"But you got her out. How?"

"If I tell you, are you going to point out that what I did was illegal?"

"Not unless someone should press charges."

Fenner listened with half an ear while Clayton told the familiar story and when he finished Bacon said with some approval:

"Very neat. You were afraid Mrs. Haskell—I believe she was your wife at one time, wasn't she?—would suffer more physical abuse?"

"That and the fact that Mark had forced her to sign a proxy for her ten percent of the company stock. If she could appear in person at the board meeting Monday she could countermand that proxy."

Bacon nodded again, his voice still easy. "Yes, I see . . . So last night you had your early dinner with Mrs. Haskell?"

"Yes. And then we went back to this apartment my friend had loaned me and talked awhile, mostly about Mark and what had happened. I'd guess I left around a quarter of ten."

"And went to your place? Just where is it, Mr. Clayton?"

Bacon noted the address, looked out the window, frowning slightly as he considered the information. When he was ready he nodded absently.

"I think I know the building. Rather old? Four or five stories?"

"Five."

"How many apartments?"

"Ten."

This time Bacon's surprise showed. "Must be large ones," he said, impressed.

"Ours—mine—is seven rooms and three baths. Half of the fourth floor."

"Automatic elevator? Doorman?"

"No. An outer and inner door. We all have our keys."

"No security?"

"At night. A guard comes on from—I think it's eleven to seven."

"But he didn't see you because you came before eleven. Did *anyone* see you?"

As Clayton said no, Sergeant Gaynor appeared in the doorway again. He coughed and said: "Monty Saxton, Lieutenant."

Bacon slipped off his perch. He thanked Clayton for coming and said he appreciated his cooperation. Clayton stood up, sighed audibly, shrugged, and walked out, gaze straight ahead and avoiding Fenner . . .

Monty Saxton was his usual dapper, jaunty self when he walked into the little room, dark eyes busy but unimpressed. He nodded coldly to Fenner, said good morning to Bacon, examined briefly the chalked outline while Bacon waited silently, making no comment. Saxton's guess as to why he was here was a good one.

"You know something, Lieutenant," he said when he was ready. "You're getting to be a nuisance. Anybody gets knocked off—and that's what this looks like—you want to talk to me."

"I know, I know," Bacon said. "A guy gets himself killed someone has to ask the questions."

"Who was it this time?"

"Jake Kinlaw."

Saxton's black brows lifted and some wariness began to work behind his eyes before he spoke.

"And you've got a theory."

"A tentative one."

"Let me tell you how it goes. Kinlaw's watching Haskell's apartment and notices something he's not ready to tell the law because he sees a chance of a score, maybe a big one. So he lies a little and propositions the killer and they make a date. Here. And he waits, maybe with a gun under the desk, and the guy surprises him because when he walks in he already has a gun in his hand. Bang, bang, bang and he walks out."

"Two bangs this time," Bacon said. "So just give me a rundown on where you were last evening from, say, eight o'clock on."

"You're not going to advise me of my rights?"

"At the proper time."

"That means you're not ready to take me in."

"You're not here under any duress, are you Monty?"

"No. The city furnished the ride. Your man said here or Headquarters, and since I'm curious I said to myself, let's see what this is all about, Monty baby."

"Yeah, yeah," Bacon said trying not to sound disgusted and only partly succeeding. "About last evening."

"You're not ready to tell me when the hit was made."

"Not yet."

"Well, I'm not ready to lay down an alibi for you just yet either, Lieutenant . . . Who the hell do you think you're questioning?" he added with increasing choler. "Some ignorant punk?"

"My apologies, Monty. I'd almost forgotten how much practice you'd had. And, you know, I sort of liked your hypothesis about Kinlaw. He put you on the scene at Haskell's and he could have lied a little about the time."

"What Kinlaw said or didn't say is hearsay now and you know it."

Bacon reddened but his voice remained level. "We haven't finished checking out the neighborhood over there yet. And those tapes Haskell made of you and your girlfriend shape up as a hell of a good motive. I doubt if he made them for fun. They were going to cost you, Monty. Maybe the tapes for his markers or he goes to your wife. Does that sound reasonable? And we haven't finished with the neighbors *here* either. So maybe you'd better think about your alibi for last night because the next time I send for you you may need your lawyer. Okay?"

"Whatever you say, Lieutenant." Saxton nodded, gave Fenner a quick slanting glance that was cool and enigmatic, and went out.

Fenner stood up. "Is that all for me, Lieutenant?"

"That's all, unless you can get lucky. You still got a client?"

Fenner chuckled and spread his hands. "Damned if I know. Maybe I'd better call Clayton and find out. I'm finished for the Moore girl."

"Well, if you want anything more from me, come up with something I can use."

17

It was warmer today, with not much breeze, and not knowing exactly what prompted his decision, Fenner told the driver to go along the Riverway. When he spotted an empty bench near the wall he told the man to stop.

The wide expanse of the river was calm and there was little activity now in late morning. On the far shore the Tech buildings stood out hazily against the sky and the several small sailboats moored there looked like toys. Later in the afternoon the eight-oared shells would be out for practice, and there would be some single shells for the aging clubmen who wanted to keep fit. Now it was quiet if one tuned out the traffic noises in the background.

He was not sure how long he sat there thinking about a lot of things but not concentrating on any one area. Rather it was more of a mental review of his own knowledge and how it related to the two deaths. The only thought that kept chasing itself around in his skull was his own uncertainty as to what he should do with the admissions Saxton had made the night before, not knowing they were being taped.

What finally brought him out of his peaceful speculation was hunger. It was after eleven when he walked back to the roadway and waited for a cab, and this time he rode to a small neighborhood eating place not far from his office. Aware that breakfast could as well serve for lunch, he ordered a half grapefruit, crisp bacon, two eggs, toast, and coffee. When he had had two cups and two cigarettes he felt better, and once at his office he asked Alice Maxwell to see if she could get Ben Clayton.

When she buzzed him a minute later Clayton was on and Fenner said: "Bacon asked me a question after you left that I couldn't answer. I thought I'd better check with you."

"What was the question?"

"Whether I still had a client. Am I still working for you or not?"

"You know something?" Clayton chuckled. "I hadn't even thought about it. I guess I assumed you were. It's a question of how long the lieutenant intends to keep me in the picture. Why don't we let it ride for a day. Maybe you can learn some things that will help and we can discuss it tomorrow."

It was after three before Fenner made up his mind about the tapes. Earlier he had talked to Marion Haskell, who informed him that Bacon had called and asked a lot of questions, some of them highly personal.

"Like how my marriage was working, and why did I leave the Dedham place, and what were my present relations with Ben. He asked about my movements last night and the night before and of course I couldn't prove that I was here both evenings. He even asked me if I owned a gun and did Mark have one. I told him I didn't but Mark did."

Now, deciding it was time to tell Bacon what had happened at his place the night before and let the police take it from there, he pushed back his chair and went into the outer office. Alice glanced up from the sweater she was knitting for her fiancé's birthday. He had been watching that sweater grow, a crew neck and heavy, and because he wanted one just like it he wondered if he could be just a little jealous of Alice's young intern. Before he could expand the thought her quick bright smile disarmed him.

"Will you be coming back?"

"Probably not," Fenner said. "I'll be at my place a few minutes and then at Police Headquarters."

"Lieutenant Bacon?"

"Right. You may as well lock up when you finish that row. Just tell the answering service I'll be in touch."

Out on the corner he debated a moment about getting his car from the parking lot, decided against it; then flagged a taxi, giving the driver his address. When, five minutes later, they pulled to the curb in front of his place, he told the man to wait.

Upstairs he rewound the tape he had made the night before. This done he opened the bedside table drawer to get the .38 he had taken from Joey. The whisky–nicotine odor was still unpleasantly noticeable as he came back through the living room. He had been too rushed by Bacon's phone call that morning to be more than vaguely aware of it and he reminded himself that when he came back he would open some windows and give the room a good airing . . .

Bacon's office door stood open. The two detectives pecking at their typewriters in the outer room gave him no more than a glance and he stopped in the doorway and leaned against the frame until Bacon looked up.

The frown was characteristic but meant nothing in particular. Fenner had telephoned from his apartment before he left to say he had something that might be pertinent. Bacon told him to bring it in. Now Bacon said: "I'm expecting somebody."

"Who?"

"The Joslin woman. A few things fell in place and I want to hear what she has to say. What have you got for me?"

"What I got is going to take some explanation and I'm not going to be rushed. Let me sit in and—"

"Going to take what sort of explanation?" Bacon said, gray eyes narrowing with doubt and suspicion.

"Well—where I got it, the circumstances, why I didn't bring it in before."

Bacon's "Hah!" was sardonic and one corner of his mouth twitched. "Why is it that with you there always has to be explanations? Just once I wish you'd come in and say, 'Here it is, Lieutenant,' and lay it on the line."

The question and comment were rhetorical and Fenner kept leaning, his gaze amused. He sensed that the lieutenant was chewing things over in his mind and could be swayed.

"I'll sit in the corner and never open my mouth. Don't forget I sort of gave you a lead on her in the first place."

"You gave me a lead on a blond. You didn't come up with any address or anything, and I'm not so sure you didn't already have it. Why do you always have to be so damn cagey?"

"I sometimes have to be in my kind of work." Fenner spoke offhandedly and now he moved to the chair by the wall. "How did you get enough to bring her in?"

"Luck . . . No!" Bacon dismissed such heresy. "Just solid, routine police work. I didn't buy her story when we talked to her the first time so we kept digging and came up with two facts that fit very neatly . . .

"Those two women schoolteachers live on the first floor. One of them has trouble sleeping, says she always was a light sleeper. So she's finally dozing off and the front door slams, the inner one. Now those old brownstones were built. Hell, the couple below Haskell didn't even hear the shots.

"So this heavy door slams," he repeated, gaze slanted upward and his clasped hands cradling the back of his neck. "The dame is annoyed as hell so she gets up and takes a peek out the front window in time to see this doll practically running down the street; and there's enough light to show it's a big girl and blond. She remembers seeing her come in once or twice a while back and she has a good idea where she's been."

He swung his chair away so he could stare out the lone window at the wall across the way and said: "Now the luck comes in because a squad car is easing along the street at just the right time. They see this blond in a hell of a hurry, and in that neighborhood, and at that hour of the morning—"

"What hour was that?"

"Around twenty of two." Bacon growled, annoyed at the interruption and made a noise that was not quite a grunt. "So the driver eases the car over to the curb to block her off at the corner and she gives them some story about being out late and trying to beat her husband home. They want to know where home is and ask for some identification. It turns out that one of the things she shows is a Louisiana driver's license. They let her go, but they remember, and when we got around to questioning the officers in that area that night, we come up with it . . . ."

He broke off as Sergeant Gaynor appeared in the doorway, made a small jerking movement of his head and stepped aside to let Sandra Joslin enter. The upward-slanting greenish eyes glanced uncertainly about as she hesitated. With her light-beige coat and a simple navy dress underneath her sexuality seemed less blatant and she lacked completely the easy self-assurance Fenner had noticed in her apartment. Bacon, on his feet with Fenner, moved the other chair near one end of the desk and waited, saying nothing, his busy eyes doing the talking. When she was seated and he had returned to his chair he allowed himself a small smile that was supposed to be reassuring.

"We need some answers, Miss Joslin," he said pleasantly, "and I have an idea you can supply them. Now we can do this one of two ways. We can talk informally and discuss certain matters here if it's agreeable to you; if not I'll hold you on suspicion and you can phone your attorney and we'll put it all on record."

A tiny frown suggested she was considering the alternatives with utmost seriousness. Her nervousness was still apparent and she crossed her legs in a practiced gesture as she hesitated. This movement revealed a lot of full and shapely thigh. She noticed it at once, remembered where she was, tugged daintily at the hem of her skirt. When she saw this attempt at modesty was only partly successful, she shrugged expressively. When she spoke her tone was listless and indifferent.

"Why not? Monty's kicking me out anyway."

"Fine." Bacon nodded encouragingly. "Now do you remember two officers in a patrol car stopping you on a street corner about a half block from Mark Haskell's place the night before last?"

"Sure."

"A lady on the first floor saw you leave the building. You had just left Haskell's flat, right. Was he dead then?"

"I don't know. I didn't touch him. I didn't kill him either."

"Did you know that he had rigged his bed with a tape recorder?"

"He told me." She jerked her chin at Fenner. "So did Monty."

"When did Monty tell you?"

Now she looked at Fenner with open resentment, the implication clear that she thought it was all his fault.

"Last night. He said he'd got it in the mail. When he got through raving he said he was throwing me out."

"You heard the three shots?"

"Yes."

"You'd been in bed before that?" When she hesitated, glance dropping, he added, exaggerating a little: "There were fresh stains on the sheet."

"Yes. We were just lying there talking."

"Had there been any interruption prior to that?"

"Once."

"How long before?"

"I don't know." Again the indifferent shoulder movement. "Maybe a couple of hours."

"What form did it take."

"Somebody was pounding on the door."

"Did Haskell answer it?"

"No. He said, you know, the hell with it. I mean, we were sort of fooling around then. Like he was getting pretty interested about that time. I guess he didn't want to have to start all over again."

"So you'd had your fun and you were lying there and it's now one-thirty or so. What happened then?"

"First the buzzer got pushed a few times and then the knocking, and by then Mark was fed up and he said he'd teach who-ever it was a lesson. He put on his robe and took this gun from the bed table and out he went."

"You stayed in bed?"

"Then, yes. I mean, I thought he'd be coming back."

"So?"

"I hear the door open and a voice says: 'Hello, Mark,' and then bam-bam-bam and the door slams." The greenish eyes were vague and unfocused now and Fenner noticed the color slowly seeping from her cheeks as the remembered shock came back to her. She had quite forgotten her parted-lips, Raquel Welch imitation, and when she seemed unaware of her silence Bacon prompted her.

"Then what?"

"Nothing. I mean, you know, I was sort of stunned and scared. I called to Mark. When there was no answer I went down the hall and peeked around the corner. There was only this one light on but I could see him on the floor. The yellow robe had come open, and I called some more, and finally got nerve enough to get closer. When I saw the blood I just panicked. Ran back into the bedroom and dressed; didn't even stop to put on my pantyhose. I got out just as fast as I could. I can't seem to remember a thing until those two cops stopped me." She looked right at Bacon then, the broad jaw tight and her eyes defiant. "And that's the truth."

Bacon gave Fenner a quick, one-eyed glance, tipped one hand. Fenner responded with some empty gesture of his own. Bacon watched silently, giving her time to calm down before he spoke.

"What about the voice?"

For a moment then she seemed perplexed. "What voice?"

"The one that said, 'Hello Mark.' Man or woman?"

"Man. But not loud. I could barely hear the words."

"Did you, or could you, recognize it? If we played some voice tapes for you?"

"I doubt it."

"Think now. You've been doing fine so don't spoil it. Was the voice Monty Saxton's?"

The "No" came automatically and Bacon said, "Sure?"

She thought a moment before she said, her indecision at once apparent: "No. I mean, no, I'm not positive. Like I couldn't swear to it. Just two words and not even loud. What do you expect?"

"All right, Miss Joslin." Bacon stood up. "Thanks for coming. You've been a big help. Now you said Saxton was kicking you out?"

"That's what he said."

"How long did he give you?"

"He said to be out by Saturday or he'd throw me out; said a lot of other things too, like what he'd do to me if I ever opened my mouth to his wife about us."

"There's just one other thing. You may not be able to leave town on Saturday. You're an important witness and we'll have to see what progress we make between now and then."

"But—you know—what will I do?" The distress showed and the eyes looked hurt. "I mean, where will I go?"

"I'd suggest a modest hotel room if you can afford it, or we could arrange for a nice cell and hold you in protective custody."

This of course was just something to say and had no sound legal ground and Bacon's sly wink told Fenner that Bacon was aware that he, Fenner, knew this. But since by then the girl was thoroughly confused she accepted it.

"All right," she said and sighed despondently. "I just hope it won't be for long. Because I have someone waiting for me back in New Orleans and I want to grab him before he changes his mind."

There was a lot of resilience here, no doubt acquired over the years by necessity, and when she uncrossed her legs and stood up she was able to smile a little, teeth again showing as her confidence returned.

"Is that all? I mean, you know, can I go?"

Bacon said she could and thanked her again for her cooperation. He stood a moment, getting a rear view of the good legs
and the shapely swinging hips and said, half to himself and half
to Fenner: "That's quite a hunk of woman."

He was still nodding absently but with approval when he
remembered that Fenner had come here for a purpose. He sat
down, head cocked and gray gaze measuring.

"Just what is this thing you've got for me that's going to take
so damn much explaining?"

Fenner took the spool of tape from his jacket pocket and
turned it over in his fingers. "Got a tape recorder that will take
this?"

Bacon spoke into the telephone and presently a man came in
with a police recorder. Fenner asked if he should thread it but
Bacon said he would. His expression as he tipped the play tab
was an odd mixture of doubt and expectancy, and now he
leaned back, pulled out a lower drawer, and hooked one foot in
the opening.

18

The expression on Lieutenant Bacon's face when the machine wound itself into silence was difficult to assess even for Fenner. He leaned forward to stop the machine, brows knotted over the bridge of his nose. After a moment he looked at Fenner and when he spoke there was an undertone of accusation in the cadence of his voice.

"How long have you had this?"

"Last night."

"How did you get Monty to open up like that and what's this about you giving somebody's piece back to him?"

Fenner slid the gun from his pocket and laid it carefully in the center of the desk, the muzzle pointing toward the door.

"I mean," Bacon continued, eyeing the gun but not waiting for a reply, "he opened up and confirmed why Haskell made the tapes and how he was going to use them if Monty didn't trade the stock assignment or what the hell ever it was he got for his IOUs and interest. I don't know how admissible this is but it confirms what we suspected and it's an A-one motive for murder; it also ties up with Jake Kinlaw and his scheme."

He leaned back again, scowling at the window. "Why should he talk to you at all?"

"I had some leverage."

Bacon looked at the gun again. "Okay, take it from the top."

Fenner got as comfortable as he could in the straight-backed oak chair and told it as well as he was able, concentrating on the proper progression from the moment Marty and Joey had stepped into his apartment.

Bacon said: "Hmm," twice, no longer doubtful but not approving either.

"I got the jump. I had to or else. I was lucky enough to get Marty across the Adam's apple and the other punk was either overconfident or a shade slow."

He went on to explain why he had smashed Joey's face, displaying neither shame nor satisfaction. By the time he had finished Bacon was on his feet, his disapproval showing. He accidentally tripped slightly over a wastebasket, glared at it, then kicked it on purpose, spilling papers on the floor. When he was ready he stooped to retrieve them, put the basket in the corner out of the way. By then his exasperation was plain.

"I'm not going to ask you why you wrecked the punk's face because that much I can understand. But why the hell did you just let the two of them walk out on you? Let Monty get the gun punk on a plane out of town? You couldn't let us in on it, could you? Give us a chance to pull them in and put the screws on, maybe involve Monty a little more?"

"What would you charge them with?" Fenner presented his argument in flat, even tones. "No breaking and entering, no unlawful entry—I let them in. Not even simple assault because they never laid a finger on me. It seemed more important to use what I had, to let it seem as if I was doing Saxton a favor in the hope that he might let his hair down a bit. He did . . . What about his alibis?" he asked in an attempt to divert the lieutenant's condemnation. "How about his poker-playing pals?"

"We've got two to admit he left the game sometime around eleven or a bit later. We can't put him on the scene at the right time yet but we haven't finished."

"What about last night?"

"Had dinner with his wife and dropped her off at his place.

That checks out. What doesn't is that he says he went to his office at Tri-State and did some work—alone. He got home around eleven. But we're still working on that . . . What time did he get to your place?"

"I'm not sure."

"Well guess, damn it!"

"Quarter of nine, maybe a bit later."

"And left?"

"I'd say nine-thirty."

Bacon stopped pacing and sat down. When his eyes came back to the gun on the desk Fenner said:

"I thought you might run that through ballistics just in case."

"We will, we will."

"It's the right caliber for Haskell. It was .38 slugs that killed him, wasn't it? This one could have been used. But not last night."

Bacon finally picked up the short-barreled gun, flipped out the cylinder to find it fully loaded. After a few seconds he pressed a button. When a detective appeared in the doorway he handed over the gun.

"Have ballistics check this out. You don't need to worry about prints. And is the sergeant out there? . . . Ask him to step in."

When Gaynor appeared Bacon pointed to the recorder. "Our friend here came up with something on his own that should help us on Saxton. On tape. Saxton not knowing it was being made. There's an especially choice statement he made about Kinlaw that I want him to hear."

Without actually doing so Bacon gave a good impression of a man wanting to rub his palms in glee.

"So let's bring him in. Officially. But not during working hours. No point in making it easy for him to get his shyster down here before we have to . . . And Joe. Let's put him in a closet for a while so we'll have time for a nice chat. Take someone with you."

Fenner had come out of his chair while the lieutenant was speaking. Now he gave a small grin, the green eyes amused.

"So much for cooperation," he said and started for the door. Before he reached it Bacon stopped him.

"Just a minute, Jackson. Come here. Sit down."

Fenner hesitated, puzzled, held by something in Bacon's face he had seldom seen, an oddly gentle look that he found impossible to diagnose. Curiosity brought him back and sat him down. Bacon gave him ten seconds of silence and now his glance strayed again to the window.

"I've been thinking," he said finally. "About that tape. We're going to play it for Saxton you know."

"It'll probably be inadmissible."

"In court yes, but not here. My point is that Saxton's going to know where we got it, and how you made it when he thought he was being confidential."

"You mean he's not going to like it," Fenner said as a faint idea began to form in some remote recess of his brain.

"I mean more than that. He's not going to like *you*. He could try to lean on you. He's done things like that before. You don't want to go around looking over your shoulder, do you?"

"Have you got an idea how I can stop him?"

"Have you? I mean, the possibility must have occurred to you."

"It did, and I have—sort of. I thought if he called me or sent someone around I'd tell him that I made a copy of that tape, that I'd delivered it to my attorney with a note of explanation, both to be turned over to Mrs. Saxton if anything happened to me."

Bacon looked back at him then, not smiling, but approval showing in the gray eyes, his faint nod complementing that approval.

"You always were a cagey bastard."

"So what do you think of it?"

"I like it, with one small modification . . . You didn't actually make that copy, did you?"

"No, but he can't know that."

"Right. So suppose *I* tell Monty about the copy and letter?

Coming from me he'll believe it. It will be official and when he realizes that the odds are stacked I have an idea he'll forget about you. He's not going to buck the two of us."

Fenner stood up, strangely moved by a suggestion so thoughtful and willingly offered. He did not know just what to say and he moved silently to the doorway before he could turn and face Bacon. The words that came then were simple.

"Thanks, Lieutenant. I appreciate it."

"Sure." Bacon smiled, not too openly but with great effectiveness. "I think I'm going to enjoy it . . . Keep in touch, hunh?"

19

Halfway to his apartment Jack Fenner realized with growing disgust that there were some unanswered questions he could have asked Bacon had he not been so absorbed in his recent spectator's role, not only as a witness to Sandra Joslin's revealing story but in the lieutenant's reaction to the new evidence involving Monty Saxton.

Now, because he hated loose ends, he redirected the cabbie whose reaction, though silent, was expressively tormented. It was no more than a four-minute detour and he did not bother to use the house phone but went directly to the elevators and along the hall to room 618 where he knocked twice, then waited hopefully until he saw the knob turn.

Barry Wilbur's dark gaze narrowed quickly when recognition came and the thick black brows bent inward with loathing. He was wearing multi-colored slacks this time and a navy turtleneck that molded nicely his lithe, well-muscled torso.

"Well, well." The sarcasm was open. "What do *you* want?"

"Just checking," Fenner said mildly. "I just came from a session in the lieutenant's office. He finally has the lead he wanted but I forgot to ask how you stand."

"What do you mean, how I stand?"

"He questioned you, didn't he?"

"You know he did. You told him I had the gun."

"So?"

"I think you also told him about my hassle with Haskell."

"I always like to cooperate with—"

"Balls!"

"Oh, for heaven's sake, Barry!" The familiar female voice cut in sharply. "Stop clowning and ask the man in."

Wilbur's apparent hostility disappeared with the command. The incipient smile that now came told Fenner that the original display of indignation might have been an act. That the smile could come at all suggested also that Wilbur felt that his troubles were behind him.

Nancy Moore was curled up in the one upholstered chair, legs tucked under her, her smile open and some new cheerfulness showing in the blue eyes.

"Hello, Mr. Fenner. Come in. We were thinking about a drink. Sit down." She indicated the other chair. "Barry can park on the bed. So what did the lieutenant have to offer?"

Fenner eyed her approvingly, liking her resilience and her quick good humor. He said he couldn't stay for a drink, but he sat down, aware that this was the first time he had seen these two together. Thinking of their suspected relationship, all of which had come secondhand, he could see how they might work things out. For this was a girl who could face life with a native intelligence and a certain worldliness and who would be unlikely to expect much more than she was entitled to. Recalling how he had once thought the word decadent might apply, he changed his mind. Now, to answer her question, he said:

"For one thing he didn't mention either of you, which would seem to indicate you were off the hook."

"We were never on it," Wilbur said from the edge of the bed. "Oh, he talked tough enough."

"Like how?"

"Like he could still charge both of us with unlawful possession of a handgun. That we were to stick around until the D.A. decided what to do about us. You know, we might have to

testify, things like that. So we planned on hanging around anyway, at least until Nancy collects. Has he got a hot lead? Does
he know who did it?"

"He thinks so."

"Who?"

"A local character who had all kinds of motive. They're pick-
ing him up now. By the way," he added casually, "where were
you last night?"

"Me? When last night?"

"Around ten or eleven."

"With Nancy, right honey?" He looked at the girl and she
nodded. "At my place," she added flatly. "I cooked him dinner
and we had a few."

"Why?" Wilbur demanded, suspicious now.

"Just asking," Fenner said.

"So did the lieutenant. Suggested we were alibiing each other
maybe. Only last night we could prove it. You got the idea he's
finally off our backs?"

"Unless you have another .38 tucked underneath the mattress."

"Not me, brother."

"How about the drink?" the girl said.

Fenner stood up. He said he would take a raincheck. Then,
cocking one brow at her he said: "I was going to phone you, but
since you're here—where do you want me to send my bill?"

The sudden digression brought an open-mouthed look before
the wry smile came and she tipped her chin.

"Oh, yes. The bill." Her gaze shifted to the window but she
spoke without resentment. "I suppose it'll be several hundred
dollars."

"Could be. I'll itemize it for you."

"Well, I really appreciate your help, and getting Kathy
Kennedy to be with me, but I'm not holding that kind of
money—"

"I can let you have it, honey," Wilbur said.

"No." She looked again at Fenner. "Send it to Mr. Tyler at

Esterbrook & Warren. Maybe he'll advance it against my inheritance if you're in a hurry."

"No hurry, Nancy. Just business. Any time it's convenient, okay?"

"Okay, if that's the way you want it." Her directness, not only in manner but the steadiness of her glance embarrassed him. To pile it on she added: "The call was strictly business? No socializing?"

The comment increased his uneasiness but he still admired her sauciness. For how could he say to this girl, *Yes. I just wanted to be satisfied that you two were clean, that bit about my bill was just a way of changing the subject.*

Unable to answer truthfully he started for the door and Wilbur went with him. He said, not looking at her, he'd see them before they left for the Coast. Wilbur said sure, and the girl said they would be in touch.

"We're not leaving," she added firmly, "until we can get together for that drink." . . .

20

It was nearly five when Jack Fenner returned to his apartment and for some unaccountable reason a sense of depression had begun to make itself felt and he was strangely dispirited. That feeling of dissatisfaction grew as the stale smells came to him and he went first to the two windows and let in some fresh air.

He was never sure why he did not let it go at that. There was good reason for the liquor smells. He and Clayton had done a lot of drinking only two nights ago, and brandy often seemed a worse offender in the area of odors. Then last night Saxton, and more drinking. Still dissatisfied he made a tour of the room looking for a glass that had been inadvertently left unrinsed.

The frown was biting more deeply into his brow when he came back to the center of the room and he swiveled his head for one more inspection. Because he was a thorough and persistent man when problems seemed to have no logical explanation he started doggedly once more in a last effort to find the source of the odor though, with the fresh air, it was now barely noticeable. Such persistence was finally rewarded and when he was satisfied he went to the telephone and made two quick calls. Lowering the windows somewhat but still leaving a one-foot open space in each, he turned and left the room.

. . .

Fenner had never been in Clayton's apartment, but recalling Bacon's questioning and Clayton's description he was prepared for something nice, and he was not disappointed. The foyer had a small Oriental on the hardwood floor and there was an antique maple table along one wall with a similar mirror above it. The medium-ceilinged living room seemed light and airy; the over-stuffed divan and chairs were both comfortable and expensive looking. There was one very large Oriental and several scatter rugs; the secretary, the wood chairs, the occasional tables looked genuine and well cared for.

To one side, through an open door, a section of a paneled, book-lined room was visible and was apparently used for a study or den; at the opposite end of the living room was a moderate-sized dining room, its elaborate and heavy-looking sideboard loaded with silver, all of it having the appearance of heirlooms.

Ben Clayton, still in his business suit, greeted him cheerfully and waved him through the foyer. He had a half-filled glass in his hand and, holding it up, said: "It's not too early for you, is it?"

Fenner said no, and asked for a Bourbon on the rocks with water. Clayton put his glass on a coaster on the coffee table, and indicated a club chair with beige upholstery. He disappeared into the study and there was a tinkle of ice cubes, a bottle neck on glass. When he came back he had an oversized old-fashion glass.

"I phoned your office first," Fenner said, accepting the drink. "They said you'd left."

"Yeah. I snuck out early today."

"Is this where you lived with Marion?"

"Yes." The thought seemed to give Clayton pleasure and the light-brown eyes came alive behind the metal-rimmed glasses. "We also bought an old—hundred and fifty years, they said— Cape Cod shingled house in Duxbury. Didn't have much in it, but a grand location and almost five acres. Had to put in a heating plant, plumbing, the works. We were doing it a little at a time." He paused then as some other memory quickly dulled his enthusiasm. "I'm still doing a bit now and then, hoping we can live there one day."

He took some of his drink and leaned back, head tilting slightly as he brought his thoughts back to the moment.

"You said you'd had another talk with the lieutenant."

"I just came from there."

"Is—is it all right to tell me what it was about or was it confidential?"

Fenner said no, settled himself, and began to recap the talk he had had, the story Sandra Joslin had told, and her status as a possible witness.

"She was there?" Clayton said in slow wonderment. "In bed when she heard the shots? No wonder she panicked. Too bad she can't recognize the voice."

"It was only two words and not loud enough for her to identify. She said it wasn't Monty Saxton's, but with her background that sort of denial would be more or less automatic."

"And you—the police too for that matter—think that this man Kinlaw actually saw the killer and threatened to tell the truth unless the killer paid off?"

"With what we know it more or less has to be that way. Furthermore Kinlaw would have to know that his man had the resources to pay."

"But wouldn't that fit any of us who were involved with Haskell? Nancy Moore didn't have much but she sure as hell was going to get a bundle."

"It wasn't a woman's voice."

"Yes. I'd forgotten." Clayton frowned, finished his drink, replaced the glass. The frown was still there and spreading around the eyes. "But—who does that leave?"

"Saxton and you, and possibly Nancy Moore's boyfriend."

"The actor fellow."

"He had a gun. The police have to consider that if he had one gun he could have two. Gun owners often have more. But unless Bacon's holding out on me, they haven't been able to tie the guy in enough to make a move."

"And that was all the lieutenant had to say?"

Fenner shook his head and sipped his drink. He said there was more and gave a somewhat expurgated account of what had happened at his apartment the night before. Because he wanted to make Clayton understand, he took his time, neither elaborating nor leaving out essential details. When he got to the part about his session with the two hoods Clayton whistled softly, eyes wide open and his voice impressed.

"Jesus!" he said, interrupting. "Didn't you take one hell of a chance, knowing this one guy had a gun?"

"It was the only chance I had." Fenner shrugged off the comment, his gaze appraising, speculating. "I knew what they had in mind for me. I'd been in spots equally bad both in and out of uniform. I also had an edge."

"Edge? In what way?"

"I knew what I had to do and they didn't. They waited a couple of seconds too long. Either from overconfidence or because they were sure they had the odds." He shrugged. "Anyway, it worked."

Clayton shook his head, still impressed. "Imagine," he said. "The Adam's apple. I never would have thought of that. And with the big guy out of the way you got the other one's gun. Then what?"

Fenner skipped the part concerning his retaliation for Joey's vicious threats but he related how he had forced Marty to phone Monty Saxton. He spoke of his hidden recorder and the conversation that followed.

"You hoped he would incriminate himself in some way?"

"I didn't know what he'd say but whatever it was, I wanted to have some corroboration—just in case."

"And you turned it over to the lieutenant this afternoon. What did he think? I mean what was his reaction?"

"He was a little miffed because I hadn't told him about the

two hoods but he got over it. He sent the sergeant out with someone to pick Saxton up."

"They'll charge him?"

"I don't know how they intend to proceed."

Clayton gave Fenner a queer, doubting look.

"You don't seem very happy about it."

"Should I be?"

"Well, from what you tell me, and the part you played, I should think you'd feel sort of puffed up about it. You certainly earned whatever you bill me for. If you, or your man, hadn't been watching Haskell's place that night you, the police too for that matter, would never have known Saxton even went there."

Fenner's grin was small and humorless. "You can take some credit for that. It was your idea in the first place that instead of trying to protect you in the customary way—a chancy thing at best—we keep an eye on Haskell in case he made some move.

"The trouble," he added after some thought, "is that this whole business is not quite as simple as it seems."

"Meaning what? If the lieutenant—"

"The lieutenant has to go by the book. And with the courts the way they are today that means practically on tiptoe. He knows that in ninety percent of the murder cases the obvious conclusion is the right one. Actually most killings solve themselves—excluding professional jobs. Frequently the thing is done out in the open with witnesses present. The victim is usually a relative, by marriage or otherwise; a friend, acquaintance. It's only now and then that murder is not what it seems on the face of it.

"Once in a while the obvious takes you up the wrong road. And if you make the mistake of following it you can lose sight of other possibilities. I think that's what Bacon is doing, and what I did. Because I could be wrong I figured he might as well see what happens with Saxton. Meanwhile I wanted to have this little talk."

Clayton seemed puzzled. He blinked once or twice, lips moving absently. His gaze was steady enough but he gave a quick shake of his head as though to clear it and spoke with a touch of disdain.

"I'm having a little trouble following you."

"You shouldn't have. You accepted the fact that Kinlaw would be wasting his time trying blackmail on someone with no capacity to pay. I've thrown out Barry Wilbur, which leaves you and Saxton. Bacon can run down his fork in the road much better than I can. So I thought I'd better explore the alternate route because I know more than the lieutenant does in this area. I also made a mistake that not only bugs the hell out of me but carries with it a touch of shame and embarrassment, a feeling I can do without."

"A mistake?" Clayton said in the same scornful tone. "In what way? If you don't mind explaining."

"I let personal considerations offset a professionalism I worked a long time to acquire and have been rather proud of. You see, Ben, I liked you. I felt you were leveling with me and for the most part you were."

He took some more of his drink and put the glass down. "I understood how you felt about Mark Haskell. I also could see how the resentment must have been building inside you over the years until it turned into a sort of loathing, directed at yourself, for having acted the toady for so long, letting Haskell's money and position, and the old man's liking for you, influence nearly everything you did.

"The catalyst, I think, was the deliberately planned setup to give your wife divorce evidence. It was a lousy thing to do, bringing her into a situation you could not explain away because you knew you were guilty and a willing partner to the scene. That was the straw. You said yourself the other night you wanted to kill him and I could understand that. But considering the background, if the desire was born then it was not something that you could forget. I think it kept building, the hate growing, the necessity to pay him back getting stronger. The recent mistreatment of the woman you still loved aggravated things. When Haskell started to threaten you, when you were supplied with a witness—Nancy Moore—who could actually substantiate those threats, you saw a way to do the job if you had some help. You got it—me."

Clayton took off his glasses and held them up to the light. When he had cleaned them with the handkerchief from the breast pocket he replaced them, settling them with thumb and index finger. When he was ready he smiled.

"You know, I really think you mean it."

"You can be sure of it. You set me up, Ben, nicely too. I had no reason not to take you at face value and that idea of watching Haskell appealed to me."

"What you're saying now is that I killed Haskell. You hope to prove it."

"I'm going to try."

"Why. Specifically?"

"For two reasons. One, I resent like hell being used by a client in any area. Murder makes it just that much worse. Any professional man takes pride in his work. When he can build a reputation in some area he wants to keep it—"

"What's number two?"

"I owe Bacon one because I held out my knowledge of the gun you brought to my place. I took precautions—I have a hunch you thought I would—and I believed you were clean. To tell Bacon would mean a lot of pressure on you and a lot of explaining and I thought, why confuse the issue? I also felt an obligation to protect any client unless it was a deliberate effort to obstruct a police investigation."

He grunted softly, an unpleasant sound. "I fell for it. That phoney drunken bit. I still don't understand all of it but you were beautiful, Ben. You really were. That calculated weaving as you stepped in, the bleary eyes, the breath, even the red face. And once I started to put it together I remembered the progression of what happened after that and how you conned me into following your script."

"If you were so sure I was guilty," Clayton said, his voice still even and unconcerned, "why come here? Why didn't you tell the lieutenant your story when you were in his office?"

"Because the missing piece didn't fall into place *until after I went home.* Without it I wouldn't even have tried to figure out the rest of it. Also I like to treat any client fairly. Until I walked in here I was working for you, remember? And don't worry, you'll get a bill. So I figured I owed it to you to tell you what I know, and what I think, so you can be ready when Bacon takes that information and begins to use it on you."

"Fair enough. I appreciate it. So go ahead."

"You made me think you were a bit loaded when you walked in. Knowing that I was supposed to be an observant, and possibly a suspicious character, you gambled I'd notice how lopsided your unbuttoned jacket was. You took pains, when you slipped that jacket over the chair back, to make sure the gun banged against the wood so I'd know something in there was hard and heavy.

"The story you then gave me would certainly increase any suspicion. Kill before Haskell kills you. I believed that part, because it was something a drunk with a grudge, and you sure as hell had one, might think of. So we both tried to do the same thing. You wanted me drunk—and I think you slipped me a little something in that last drink—so I'd be out for a few hours. I wanted you out to protect you from your drunken fantasy.

"You knew I'd had one drink and maybe two. You demanded brandy and you got it"—his chuckle was abrupt and mirthless —"but not my best. You insisted I have one. We drank and talked. You told me all about your toady days, the paid companionship; about Haskell's plan, with that public relations guy's help, to get the girls and play strip poker that night. You even admitted that you might have tumbled into bed with your partner if Haskell hadn't arrived with your wife."

He paused and said: "It all made sense, especially coming from a drunk. So when you demanded a final drink, I slugged it good. A bit later you insisted I have one to accompany you and

I humored you, figuring that keeping you on the sofa all night was worth a hangover. I also remember that you were just finishing yours—or so I thought—when I came back into the room. Actually you were just putting the glass down with a sip or two in it—I guess you slipped me whatever it was while I was in the kitchen . . . You with me so far?"

"Very much so, Jack. I find it fascinating."

"Around about that time you go to the john, gambling, and you were right, that I'd check the gun just in case. I dumped the slugs and felt better. I got the blanket and pillow and you said, no heel taps, so I swallowed the spiked drink and took off for bed. You want me to guess what you used?"

"Why not?"

"I have a prescription for sleeping capsules both Nembutal and Seconal. I maybe use one three or four times a month. But the Nembutal only when I've had a couple of tough nights before and deliberately take one. Because they work more slowly and the effects last longer. I don't like the morning-after feeling. Seconal I can get up and take and it works in twenty or thirty minutes and lasts, with me, maybe four hours or so with no after effects at all. For you time didn't matter. All you needed was a safe hour, or less—you could walk to Haskell's in ten minutes from there.

"So I woke up just before dawn. Scared. Thinking you just might possibly have snapped out of it long enough to go looking for Haskell with an empty gun. When I found you right where I'd left you I went back and slept some more."

He paused to get a cigarette. Clayton took one of his own filters and offered a light from the familiar silver Zippo.

"But the thought of that gun still bothered me even though I had the shells. Because I couldn't exclude the possibility that you had extra ones in your pants. So while you were using my electric razor I checked it."

"Was it still empty?" Clayton's tone was that of an adult encouraging a child.

"It was."

"Clean?"

"Very. Except for one spot of corrosion that had been there a long time. Clinging to that rough part were a couple of tiny bits of lint, like little tufts. But the barrel was clean and shiny and that was enough for me."

"But not any longer?"

"Not any longer."

"Are you saying that while the gun was clean in the morning I used it on Mark earlier. How could that be?"

"It took some thinking. Since by then I was convinced I'd been manipulated there had to be a way. You could say it was a mental exercise in trial and error."

He paused again, the green gaze bleak, "If you used it—and by then I was sure you had—it had to be cleaned. I couldn't see you carrying a cleaning rod and oil can in your pants pockets —and I'd searched your coat. And it was that that gave me a clue."

"I'm not sure I follow. What I had in my jacket pockets tipped you off. How?"

"You had one of those cheap, small-diameter French pens. It could easily be used as a makeshift cleaning rod for a .38 . . . I have to guess now but try it for size, hunh? If you had a cleaning cloth, or if you'd cut a piece out of, say, your handkerchief there might possibly be some threads caught on that corroded spot, but not lint. Lint could easily come from cotton. Lighter fluid would serve as a cleaning solvent even though it wouldn't be as protective as oil . . . Are you with me so far?"

"Definitely," Clayton said and this time there was no patronizing humor in his tone.

"So where would you get a saturated hunk of cotton that could be an effective cleaning cloth and agent. I imagine you've had that silver Zippo some time, right? And you used it to light my cigarette that first morning in George Tyler's office. You lit me one the night you set me up; you just gave me another light. But yesterday morning when you came from the bathroom you sparked that Zippo three times and gave up, remember?

"The wick was dry, right, Ben? Because you had used that saturated cotton filling to get a clean and shiny gun barrel. Beautiful. Perfect in fact if I hadn't already been suspicious . . . I assume you repacked the lighter back in your office because you just proved it was in working order again."

Not sure just what the reaction would be, Fenner put his cigarette out and leaned back, his gaze more watchful than speculative.

It took some seconds to get any facial response and even then it was somewhat ambiguous. There may have been a trace of shock in the bespectacled eyes, some unease at least; possibly just a trace of respect. When Clayton finally spoke his voice was low and thoughtful.

"That's a damn fine hypothesis. When did you figure it all out?"

"I got it maybe a half hour ago when I realized for sure I'd been taken for a ride."

"And what made you so sure?"

"For one thing I have, always have had, a good sense of smell. When you left my apartment the next morning it had the same stale, boozy smell you get in bars before they are aired out. It meant nothing then, the explanation for it simple enough. I noticed it some last evening but Saxton and his boys kept me too occupied to wonder much about it. Then this morning Bacon got me up and out in a hurry and I had no time to speculate.

"But this afternoon when I'd come back from Headquarters I'd had enough of it. I could have aired the place out and let it go at that but sometimes I'm stubborn, Ben. I like answers. So I started looking to see if there were unwashed glasses around. When I couldn't find any I just kept looking, annoyed somehow that I couldn't find a proper reason . . . Did you know that spilled brandy makes a worse stain than, say, whisky?"

He paused, watching the change come and sensing the effort it took to control the mask that had settled over Clayton's face.

"You had to get rid of that last drink I made. With what you already had you knew you might not make it to Haskell's if you drank it. But there were no convenient vases or flower pots, so you tossed nearly the whole glassful as far back under the davenport as you could reach. It was dry all right when I finally discovered it a little while ago. The odor wasn't too noticeable then either but it had been. And the stain." He let out a small sigh and shook his head. "A sort of silent witness, you know? I'd spilled brandy before. Once on a pair of light-colored slacks. Never did quite come out in spite of several cleanings."

Clayton had been listening with obvious interest. Now, showing no outward concern, he seemed almost to approve of such reasoning.

"How about that?" he said softly. "One lousy mistake, hunh?"

"That was the important one."

"Funny." Clayton let the remark pass. "I thought it might be weeks before it was discovered. Didn't think about a stain or any special smell . . . And speaking of drinks, I could use one. I'm getting damn dry." He stood up lazily. "Fix one for you?"

When Fenner said he would coast, Clayton nodded and moved into the study, and once again the ice sounds came.

21

When he came back to the living room Ben Clayton went to sit in a corner of the divan, which put him roughly five feet from Fenner. He took an appreciative swallow, put the glass on an end table at his elbow, and leaned back, his hands at ease. Then, out of nowhere, he came back to the remark that Fenner assumed had gone unnoticed.

"You said that was my important mistake," he said, eyes guarded and sleepy-looking. "What was the other?"

"There could be more than one; there usually is. If so Bacon will probably turn them up before he's through. But what I was referring to, and still don't understand, is why the hell you took the chance of going to Haskell's when you must have realized that Kinlaw might still be there."

"It wasn't quite that way, but we can come back to that. Still, I can see you're convinced I went there."

"What else? If Kinlaw hadn't seen you he couldn't put the finger on you. He'd still be alive. You killed Haskell for reasons I can understand. Plenty of guys have been killed for a hell of a lot less. But Kinlaw was deliberate, cold-blooded, and unnecessary, at least at that time. How much did he want?"

He saw the lazy rolling movement of Clayton's hips as he finished. By the time the buttocks had settled back in place the gun was in Clayton's hand, pointing, but with no visible pressure on the trigger. Then, as the silence grew, Fenner took time to analyze his thoughts.

There was, he knew, some area of honest surprise but it was not overwhelming. Mixed with this was an odd sense of satisfaction, not just because his judgment and actions had been vindicated but because he had been able to take a few seemingly minor details and make them add up. True, there had always been some small lingering doubt in the back of his mind, the nagging worry, like a small burr not yet beginning to fester, that he could have been an unwilling participant in a really clever murder scheme. That he could dismiss or crowd back the possibility that Clayton was guilty was due to a lack of even minor evidence or a single fact that would support such doubt.

Now, bringing his mind back to the moment, giving the revolver but a quick glance, he looked right at Clayton, his grin tight, fixed, and twisted.

"What do you expect to do with that?" he asked mildly.

"I'm not quite sure but I have a couple of things in mind. I'm going to buy a little time, but first—stand up and keep your hands still!"

"Stand up? Sure if you say so."

"Now take your jacket off."

When Fenner had complied, holding the garment in one hand, Clayton told him to turn round.

Fenner did so, saying, "No gun, Ben."

"I imagine you own one."

"Two as a matter of fact, one home and one at the office. I even thought about bringing one with me but this isn't TV. There, if you kept count, any given private dick will kill maybe forty, fifty bad guys during a season, all apparently without a serious investigation. With me, I even fire a gun, regardless of circumstances or provocation, my license is suspended pending a hearing."

"I imagine you've used a gun?"

"Not since I've been on my own."

"Been shot at?"

"A few times. I've got a scar on my rib cage to prove one of them. You want to see it?"

Clayton ignored the sarcasm. "Actually," he said, still calm and with some unexpected connotation of amusement, "I wasn't thinking about a gun. What I had in mind was maybe a miniature recorder so you could do to me what you did to Monty Saxton last night. Because I sort of get the idea you plan on turning me in, right?"

"Something like that."

"Why? I mean, you're still working for me . . . Never mind. You can put your jacket on. And sit down, please."

When Fenner had eased back on the chair he said: "I think I told you why I have to turn you in."

"To keep your self-respect for letting me use you?"

"And to keep Bacon from banning me from Headquarters. A private investigator can't work without contacts. I need favors from my friends in the department from time to time. I try to do what I can in return. When Bacon finds out I kept my knowledge of your gun from him he's going to get purple and walk stiff-legged and give me hell and threaten to charge me with this and that—until he begins to understand why I was suckered, that the gun was clean, and that I had some obligation to you, or any other client, under the circumstances. Then he'll sulk a while, but he'll finally have to admit I helped crack the case and things will be okay again. Understand?"

"Perfectly. And that's why I wanted to be sure about any recorder. Talking like this, with no witnesses, I can explain a thing or two. It'll be just your word against mine and that sort of testimony on your part wouldn't be worth a dime. Or am I wrong?"

"You're probably right."

"So let's get the Kinlaw thing straight. I wasn't quite so stupid as you make me appear."

"Oh?"

"Once I'd made up my mind to kill Mark—and I made that

decision when he started to abuse Marion—I began to explore the possibilities. I wasn't sure when but, as you said, his threats helped decide me because, believe it or not, he was really cracked enough to try to get to me one way or another.

"But as I said, I'd started to plan before that. Without knowing just how I could work it I decided it might be well to have a key to the back door of that building, just in case. You met— at least you've seen—the super? . . . A boozer, right? So I looked him up a couple of weeks ago. I bought a stage mustache and put on dark glasses, and wore a hat, something I seldom do . . . Are you with me so far?"

He watched Fenner nod and said: "We had a couple of drinks together and I fed him a story about wanting to get some evidence about a cheating wife. I said I thought she was seeing Haskell once in a while, and I wanted to be able to sneak up the back way some night and surprise her. I pointed out there was no risk because I'd never admit making an illegal entry and he'd never give me away because then I'd have to tell the truth and he'd lose his job."

Fenner listened with mounting interest. It was, he saw, a rather neat idea and while pieces began to fall in place he wanted the rest of it.

"He bought it?"

"When he saw a new fifty-dollar bill. For an extra key—if he had one—or a duplicate if he didn't, another fifty."

He gave other details but Fenner was no longer interested in such things and waited until Clayton got back to the specific incident that concerned Jake Kinlaw. It came a few seconds later.

"If your man Kinlaw hadn't decided to goof off for a while he'd still be alive. But he did. And, not wanting to get caught doing it out there on the street, he drove round to the alley behind the building and parked to have a little snooze for himself. I don't remember if there was a moon that night or not. If there was it must have been partial and quite well down. But there were stars and I could see fairly well, except the floor of the alley."

He took a small breath and said: "What I didn't see was a couple of trash cans. I bumped into one and rattled it a bit. I saw the parked car up ahead. There was no movement, no lights, and I couldn't see anyone in it. So when it got quiet again I just kept going."

"You thought the Joslin woman had left by then?"

"I didn't care if she had or not. When he opened the door I was going to shoot. I hadn't planned to say anything. The 'Hello Mark' just slipped out but not loud. It didn't worry me."

"And Kinlaw saw you?"

"Exactly."

"When did he get in touch with you?"

"The next morning. After he learned what had happened to Mark. He knew I had to be the one so he got me at the office."

"Personally?"

"By telephone. He identified himself, told me what he wanted. All he asked for was a quick yes or no."

"How much did he ask?"

"Five thousand plus three hundred a month for life. He said he wasn't greedy but could use another pension. He told me where to come and when. If I didn't bring the five thousand with me before midnight he'd know what to do."

"I can guess the rest of it," Fenner said, his green gaze brooding now, the disgust and growing resentment held in check.

"He had a gun," Clayton said.

"And little chance to use it. You never intended to pay."

"Would you have?"

"You could afford it. You were getting the equivalent of three quarters of a million shortly—"

"Answer my question!"

"Isn't it all pretty academic now?"

"I want to know."

"All right. Yes, I think I would have if I could have raised that five."

"And kept paying, knowing he could up the monthly payment until he was bleeding me?"

"You forget I knew Jake better than you did. I think he would have been satisfied with that monthly payment. For me it would be good insurance. And he would know something that you did not consider. Once the arrangement got going there was little he could do safely except to bluff. He could phone the authorities anonymously, which would do no good except to subject me to fresh questioning. Because tips won't stand up in court. To come out with his evidence would immediately make him an accessory to murder, and accessories can wind up with a rather long sentence, not to mention the extortion rap. Knowing this, and at his age, I think he'd have been very happy with that nice easy three hundred a month for life."

He held up his hand to forestall the coming interruption. "*But* if what you imagined happened did happen, if he started upping the demands, it would be time enough to consider the alternative. I'm damn sure I'd have waited until the Haskell case cooled off. *If* I thought I had to kill I'd have picked a better time, and place and method."

"Sure," Clayton said with heavy sarcasm. "But you're smarter—"

"Not smarter, Ben. Just more experienced. With Haskell you had a neat, premeditated, well-thought-out plan with an almost perfect alibi—me. You thought when I confirmed that alibi—and damned if I didn't do just that—that you'd be above and beyond suspicion. Perhaps you would have, except for that loaded drink you had to get rid of one way or another the best you could.

"But Kinlaw," he added with an absent shake of his head, "that was no way to kill, Ben. What you should have known, or realized if you hadn't panicked, was that what you needed most was time. Me? I think I'd have looked around a bit first. I'd have made some contacts. For a thousand or so I think I could have found someone who could do a nice hit-and-run job with a stolen car where, even if caught, it would be almost impossible to wind up with more than involuntary manslaughter or vehicular homicide. A good man would never even be suspected. It's an old standby that's been used over and over because it is so difficult to prove intent when done by a stranger. But what's the point in spelling it out? It's only conjecture now, isn't it?"

"Yeah. Oh, that sounds great, just great," Clayton said bitterly. "But you weren't scared. I was. You were never in my spot; you can't know what it's like to feel the panic building in you."

"Sure."

"I had no regrets for Mark Haskell," Clayton went on as though he had not heard. "He had it coming. I knew he would never be able to hurt me or Marion again. I thought I had done well. I was sure I could get away with it. And then this cheap bloodsucker spoils everything. If he hadn't been a thief—"

"If he hadn't been, you'd be in a cell now." Fenner paused; then digressed to a point that had been bothering him. "Tell me something. How did you get as far as Kinlaw's desk? I mean, that's where he was shot. You had to go all the way through the living room—"

"Oh." Clayton, who had started to squint, now understood the question. "I couldn't shoot when he opened the door. It was different with Mark. I knew what I wanted to do that time. This time I wasn't sure. And there were too many apartments around—"

"He opened the door for you. Did you see a gun? Did you have yours out?"

"No. Mine was in my waistband, the jacket buttoned—because I still didn't know what was going to happen. He was watching me pretty closely and we went back to the desk and he sat down and asked about the money. I knew then what I had to do. I took out the bills—not five thousand but enough to make it look good—and put them on the desk with my left hand. When he reached for them he forgot to watch me. When he did see my gun he came up with his, from the desk drawer I think. And I pulled the trigger and so did he but my shot had hit first and must have spoiled his aim and I pulled the trigger again."

Fenner nodded, understanding now, and leaned forward so that his hands were on his kneecaps. That brought his eyes less than four feet from the gun. He gave it a close and narrow-eyed inspection before he looked again at Clayton. Then, because he wanted to know all he could, he changed the subject.

"What was it you put in my drink, Ben?"

Suspicion had begun to show in Clayton's bespectacled eyes. The face that Fenner had once thought vague and distracted and guileless had hardened.

"Is that relevant now?"

Fenner lifted one hand idly, dropped it back on the kneecap. To disguise his true feelings he put on what he thought was a look of indifference. Because he wanted Clayton to keep talking while he decided just how to play it he said:

"Maybe not, Ben. But humor me? It wasn't a regular Mickey; not chloral hydrate or I'd have been groggy when I woke up instead of feeling fairly alert considering the booze I'd put away."

"You had it right the first time."

"Seconal?"

"Because it acts on me just as you said it did on you. It bothered me a bit, knowing how much to use. I'd read that a heavy mixture of alcohol and barbiturates could be fatal. I counted on being able to get a couple of drinks into you; I knew you'd had one before I came."

"So?"

"So I took three capsules and split them right here before I left. Dumped the powder into a bit of toilet paper and folded it, carrying it in my handkerchief. I guessed that not all of it would be ingested and the color of your drink plus the ice cubes would make the undissolved particles unnoticeable. Later, before I went out, I rinsed my glass, leaving a bit of water to take care of the unmelted ice."

"Neat," Fenner said dryly. "You thought of everything, even the proper dosage."

"Almost everything." Clayton spoke with some bitterness and his face had become impassive, wooden. "George Tyler said you were about the best in town. He said you were smart, competent, and honest. I guess I should have hired some hack."

He jerked the gun muzzle an inch or two to get Fenner's attention, repointed it.

"If I let you walk out of here you'll call the lieutenant?"

"Under the circumstances I have no choice."

"And what would you guess my chances are if I do—I mean in court?"

"With that," Fenner said, indicating the gun, "not too good. Why didn't you dump it while you could?"

"I thought about it. In fact I intended to when I got the right chance. Then I got the call from your man Kinlaw. After that —I don't know—maybe I was afraid I'd need it again with my luck running the way it was. Maybe I thought about using it on myself if I had to."

He took a large breath and let it out slowly, a look of discouragement clouding his gaze. "With this I have no chance, is that it?"

"You'll have plenty of dough for the best counsel. Maybe murder two; maybe even manslaughter. Deals are made. Pleas are arranged; too damn many for my taste. And even if the judge and jury lay it on you—if your attorney is tricky enough —the Supreme Court may overturn the conviction. To get convicted nowadays, and make it stick, you need more than unimpeachable witnesses and sound evidence. If you had thought a bit more about Kinlaw—"

"Don't preach to me now, Jack."

"I was about to say that with only Haskell, and him holding a gun, it might have been manslaughter, possibly suspended. But okay. So what *are* you going to do with that gun?"

"Suppose you give me a little time. Why don't you finish your drink while you have the chance?"

22

The time Ben Clayton asked for amounted to no more than two minutes. During that interval nothing changed in his face; only the eyes remained troubled. Fenner sat where he was, finishing his drink as directed and not yet ready to force the issue.

Then, quite abruptly, Clayton seemed to pull himself together, squaring his shoulders some and rearranging his features purposefully. His voice when he finally made his ultimatum was quiet but level.

"I'm going to give you a choice. I can use this—why not, what do I have to lose now?—or you can let me lock you in a closet for twenty minutes, maybe less, while I duck out and get rid of this. I'll then come back and release you and you can go right ahead and make your damn call."

Fenner looked again at the gun and let his eyes slide up until they met Clayton's. Slowly then, almost regretfully it seemed, he shook his head.

"Sorry Ben. I just never learned to play that way. You had a damn nice plan, even down to every detail but one."

"You mean the brandy thing?"

"Plus the bad luck of running into Kinlaw, who should never have been where he was in the first place. But those are the

breaks. Not getting philosophical on you, we both know everyone gets breaks, some good, some bad. No one escapes. You did
what you set out to do. Good God, man! You're intelligent
enough to realize that any plan, no matter how clever, has some
chance of going bad. You had to know there was a possibility
you'd get caught in spite of everything.

"I told you before and I'll say it again: that act you put on
when you came to my place the night before last was beautiful.
That phoney weaving and the bleary eyes—"

The digression seemed to arouse some interest. "I rubbed the
hell out of them before I came upstairs. All I had to do was keep
blinking and try to keep them from focusing now and then."

"But the red face?"

"I dug out a shirt a half-size too small; damn near choked
getting it on, felt choked until I loosened it."

"How many drinks *did* you have. Your breath—"

"Just one. To get up enough nerve to come at all. But I had
a flask in the glove compartment of my car. I took a mouthful
when I left it down the street, held it there until I saw your
lights on and knew you were home." He shrugged, his faint
smile wistful at the memory. "I just swallowed when you
opened the door and blew it in your face."

"All right. You took your best crack. The odds just caught up
with you. So take your medicine, get some high-powered legal
help. Shooting me isn't going to help you now or solve anything.
So why not give me that gun and get on with what has to be
done?"

He had been moving slowly, almost imperceptibly, as he
spoke. First the hands came off the kneecaps; then he leaned
forward still more, feet placed so he could rise quickly, his right
hand beginning to reach.

Clayton's reaction, when he realized what might happen, was
not surprising. Almost automatically his body recoiled and stiff-
ened, the gun retracting with the movement, his stare aghast
with a spasm of alarm.

"No!" he said harshly, "Don't! I mean it! Please, Jack. Don't make me."

Fenner hesitated, narrowed gaze fixed on Clayton and seeing now the finger pressure, the slow movement in the gun as the cylinder started to revolve and the hammer retracted. It stopped halfway as Clayton cried:

"Don't make me do it!"

"Then don't!" Fenner snapped, his voice flat and demanding. "What the hell are you trying to prove? Afraid to take your chances with the law? Will it make you feel any better, killing me for doing my job?"

The hammer stayed where it was and so did Fenner. When he saw the indecision as his words struck home he said:

"You gave me two choices. Now I'll give you two. Hand over the gun or lay it nice and gentle on that table next to your drink."

The collapse came then, a little at a time, the muzzle dipping as the shoulder started to sag. The lights went out of the bespectacled eyes and the chin came down. The gun hand got limp and started to dip, inch by inch until it touched the cushion between his thighs. The sigh that followed was both visible and audible. For five seconds he seemed to be looking at the gun as though he had never seen it before. Finally he lifted it, reached out, and placed it on the table.

When he looked up the fear and wonderment were still in his tortured gaze. "I could have killed you, Jack. I almost did."

"No," Fenner said and picked up the gun. "I'll show you why."

As he spoke he flipped out the cylinder. There was one shell there and he moved it where he wanted it. He pointed it directly at Clayton.

"You're not very familiar with guns, are you Ben?"

"That's the only one I ever owned. Just used it that one time for target practice. Why? What's to know? You just load it and pull the trigger."

"I thought so. And mostly you're right. But look right at this one. Go ahead, Ben. Study the cylinder. It's open at your side. Tell me what you see."

The eyes, at first uncomprehending, grew fixed. When Clayton finally glanced up the brow was furrowed.

"There's a bullet in one of these holes, the others I can see are empty."

"I was close enough to see all I had to see." Fenner sat down and relocated the shell. "The two on each side were empty, which meant there could be no more than two slugs in the gun, either at six o'clock or twelve o'clock. Understand?"

When Clayton nodded Fenner continued: "Where was the gun originally?"

"In the Duxbury place. I brought it here about ten days ago."

"Did you bring a full box of shells?"

"It wasn't full. I'd used most of them in practice a long time ago. I didn't count them, just took what I had because I knew there were enough."

"I removed the six you brought to my place," Fenner said. "The rest were in your pants pocket. You used three on Haskell and two on Kinlaw, which means there must have been twelve altogether."

"I still don't understand—"

"If the live slug was at six o'clock you'd have to pull that trigger three times to put it under the hammer. There was no way you could make it before I could stop you. Twelve o'clock, six times."

"Oh."

The understanding that he had never had a chance came to Clayton slowly and presently the anger and resentment began to show. "Then why the hell did you do it that way? Why didn't you just take it away from me? Why grandstand like that? Was there any point or did you just want to humiliate me?"

"There was a point, Ben," Fenner said and now his tone was gentle. "I had to know. If you had pulled that trigger I would have reported it that way. More important to me, I would also have known that you didn't deserve a break."

Clayton said: "Oh—" again.

"I'll have to make a statement to Bacon and the D.A.'s office and probably later on the witness stand. I gave you a chance and you didn't take it. So now I can state, and without lying, that though you still had a live shell in that gun and could have fired, you didn't. That might not help you much but it could be better than nothing."

"And if there *had* been shells, Jack?"

Fenner shrugged. "Then I'd have had to try some other way, wouldn't I?"

He slipped the revolver into a hip pocket, his tone once again businesslike.

"Is there a phone in the den?"

"Yes." The voice was low and full of gloom.

"The booze too? Because this may be our last chance for quite a while . . . Come on. You can make me a fresh one too."

Clayton put his hands on his knees and pushed erect. When he had straightened his shoulders he moved toward the open door without hesitation.

Once inside he busied himself with the glasses and Fenner glanced at his watch, surprised that he had been here so short a time. His knowledge of Kent Murdock's habits made him hopeful that the photographer would still be at his office, and he was right.

When he had the number he said what he had to say and Murdock was not one to argue away a chance at a picture even though most of his work these days was inside.

When Clayton realized what was happening he protested. "That was a lousy thing to do. Why the hell do you have to call the newspapers in? Do you need publicity that bad?"

"No publicity," Fenner explained patiently. "I mean for me. It's bad for business. But Kent Murdock helped me some. He's helped before and I hope he will again. I like to reciprocate when I can. He'll be here, alone, when the lieutenant gets here. I don't think Bacon will object; why should you? It's better for you than facing the newspapers *and* maybe the TV guys down at Headquarters isn't it?"

Clayton shrugged, his face sullen now as he turned to the drink tray. Fenner made his next and last call but had less luck reaching Bacon. The detective he talked to said the lieutenant was out but could be reached. As he gave the message, Fenner decided it was better this way. Had he been connected directly he would have had to argue some because Bacon was not one to honor vague requests from private investigators unless he could be convinced they were unusually important!

Clayton had the Bourbon-on-the-rocks ready when Fenner replaced the telephone. The broad face was grave and thoughtful but no longer either resentful or embittered. He had, somehow, accepted the situation as inevitable and his whole mood suggested that he was more resigned than discouraged.

Such an attitude demanded a certain respect and Fenner acknowledged it as he stepped round the desk and eased wearily into the chair. There was, he knew, an awful lot about Ben Clayton that he liked, and the pervasive feeling that came over him took the form of a slow awareness of his own physical and mental exhaustion rather than any feeling of satisfaction. He took a swallow of his drink and was grateful. Then, seeing Clayton still standing uncertainly with the handset in his hand, he asked what the matter was.

"I don't know who to call."

"Esterbrook & Warren. The answering service will tell you where George Tyler is and if you can't get him talk to any partner. Tell him you want the best criminal lawyer in town and right now. If he can't meet you here in fifteen or twenty minutes tell him to meet you at Headquarters . . . You know, Ben," he added, trying to keep it light, "it's going to be easier for you tonight than me."

"How the hell is it?"

"Me, I've got an awful lot of talking to do, much of it repetition . . . You, you can stand mute. All you have to tell Bacon is your name, address, and occupation. After that your lawyer does the talking . . . Come on, fellow, get on with it."

He slouched back in the chair again, stretching his legs, hearing vaguely the conversations that followed. When he finally found a comfortable position he concentrated only on trying to keep his mind completely blank.

George Harmon Coxe was born in Olean, New York, and spent his youth there and in nearby Elmira. After a year at Purdue and one at Cornell, he worked for five years with newspapers in California, Florida, and New York, and did advertising for a New England printer for five more. Since that time he has devoted himself to writing—for two years with Metro-Goldwyn-Mayer, then as a free lance, selling numerous short stories, novelettes, and serials to magazines as well as to motion-picture, radio, and television producers.

He is a past president of the Mystery Writers of America, and winner of its Grand Master Award in 1964.

A Note on the Type

This book was set in Gael, the computer version of Caledonia, designed by W. A. Dwiggins. It belongs to the family
of printing types called "modern face" by printers—a term
used to mark the change in style of type letters that occurred about 1800. Caledonia borders on the general de-
sign of Scotch Modern, but is more freely drawn than that
letter.

This book was composed, printed, and
bound by The Haddon Craftsmen, Inc.,
Scranton, Pa.